The Shoemaker

MARK SABA

CASA LAGO PRESS
NEW FAIRFIELD, CT

Diaspora
Volume 7

As "diaspora" is the dispersion or spread of people from their original homeland, this book series takes its name in the intellectual spirit of willful dispersion of subject matter and thought. It is dedicated to publishing those studies and creative works that in various and sundry ways either speak to or offer new methods of analysis and/or articulations of the Italian diaspora.

The publication of this book has been made possible through a generous grant from an anonymous donor who wishes not to be identified but urges others to donate to historical and cultural studies.

ISBN 978-1-955995-12-2
Library of Congress Control Number: Available upon request

CASA LAGO PRESS
New Fairfield, CT

In memory of my grandmother

Caterina Tavolieri

TABLE OF CONTENTS

The Shoemaker

Mark Saba

*Chi si volta, e chi si gira
sempre a casa va a finire.*

CHAPTER 1

FROM A HILLTOP THAT OVERLOOKED OTHER HILLS east of the city, as well as the valleys of two opposing rivers, they gathered to mourn the death of their father, Pietro Cavalieri. The youngest stayed well behind their black-clad elders, leaving the business of grieving to them, who bore that responsibility almost wholly for their beloved matriarch, Almerinda Marchionna-Cavalieri. For privately they believed the old man to be a son-of-a-bitch.

"Pete! Pete! Perchè tu m'hai lasciato?" she wailed, asking the heavens once again why, and receiving for an answer only the simple, saddened faces of her progeny. She knew then, finally, that they could never share her grief, because they had not known Pietro in the way she had.

After the old priest had finished his prayers and a strong gust of fall wind had blown his prayer book shut, Pietro felt the first clods fall into the pit and onto his casket. "When I die," he'd told his wife more than once, "just tie me into a sack and throw me in the river. Don't waste our money." It was just one of the many things he'd thrown out to her in a fit of crazed conviction, partly brought on, she'd thought, by the troublesome and unconventional course their lives had taken. She almost always found it in her heart to forgive him, even when he wouldn't speak to her for weeks at a time. But even that didn't begin until they had become established in America, in the soot-blackened town that contained every despicable nationality on Earth except the French: the only ones he considered on par with the Italians.

"But Pete, look, we have plenty of food to eat in America, and a promise for our children's children," Almerinda would implore. After the expected time-independent scowl he would deign to answer:

"And all we have to do is live here in hell."

3

It was customary for them to disagree in silence, for Almerinda knew she was no match for his wit. Often it took a family crisis to get them to speak to one another again. This time, lying in his casket, Pietro did the forgiving. He forgave Almerinda for putting him through this, because he knew now that she did it to honor the family. If he were still alive, he would speak to her; he would tell her this. But it was too late for words. All that he had left her was the words he had already spoken, and the feelings that had left him through his eyes, mouth, and hands on their way to her heart. As the clods of cool Pittsburgh earth fell over him, he gave up contact with the living, and gave up his soul to meet the dead. His last impulse went directly to his beloved Almerinda, who began to tremble from head to toe, while whispering *"Addio, Pete – ti sento pian piano come un angelo."* Having spoken these words she regained her composure, stood quietly for a moment, and turned to lead them back down the hill to their cars.

Inside the casket Pietro's former body lay straight and still, but not perfect—the undertaker had carelessly positioned his tie askew, though no one had dared to straighten it. For that crooked tie, unknown to the funeral home staff, had been Pietro Cavalieri's trademark; along with an unevenly shaven face, nicked fingers, and a pair of cowlicks that had followed him even into old age, and now into the grave.

During the drive back to the house Almerinda kept her window tightly shut, while her eldest daughter Pina, now forty-eight years old, rolled hers down even further than she would have if her mother hadn't been in the car.

"Pina, close the window. I feel a draft everywhere today."

Pina, half lost in her own reverie, virtually ignored Almerinda's comment until her husband spoke up:

"Pina! Listen to your mother."

That was a cry she'd heard all too often in her life, and more often than not from her father. She rolled the window up for her *babbo*, but left it open a slight crack, also for him. He too appreciated fresh air. Almerinda, predicting her daughter's every move, turned to face her. Pina's impulse was to stare her down, but finally she succumbed, rolling the window up tightly, while forcing out a sigh that could have sent shivers down a mad dog's spine. Almerinda wiped her eyes again with her embroidered handkerchief, as Pina felt her heart rising to her throat from having to endure such theatrics.

"Leave her alone," Pietro warned her. "She'll work it out. Don't look at me that way! It's not my fault I died. Have some respect for your mother. If you are pretty it's because of her." It was just like him, thought Pina, to say something like that safely after he'd died. Everyone knew she resembled her father: pointed eyebrows, full eyes, Roman nose, the expressive lips. Her hair was not black but chestnut-colored, and her eyes (though some saw flashes of color in them) gray. She'd never noted the color of her mother's eyes, but she knew her father's had been brown — not deep and alluring brown, but brown like the earth and the trees: earth-brown, for he was of the earth. Whatever he was could be read plainly in his eyes. He was the same before everyone, and she was sure now that her father put on no pretense while meeting the Almighty.

This is not to say that she revered him; more than once she had denounced him, either *sottovoce* or loud enough for her mother to hear. And her mother, beneath that veneer of healthy good looks and generous charm, had eyes of steel. They saw through everything with their clear sky color and endless depth. When Pina heard her full name leaving her mother's lips, its four hard syllables in somber monotone — *Giu-sep-pin-a* — she knew the woman was on to something. It was the same tone she used to introduce a serious topic of discussion to her husband: *Pi-e-tro*.

5

Senti! Pietro rarely listened, and it was Almerinda's insistence that he should that had annoyed Pina. She was now beginning to feel that things would be different around the house, that Almerinda's supplications would have to be redirected to someone else. Pina vowed that it would not be her. She was also very good at not listening.

Giuseppina and Jim (he insisted on Anglicizing his non-native-sounding name, Giacomo) had once lived on the second floor of her parents' house: a modest red-brick, federal style, with a shallow front yard and deeper back, lined on either side by a rusting wire fence against which either tomatoes, zinnias, peppers, or curly endive grew. Pina also harvested their wild dandelions for salad. Almerinda denounced this practice, suggesting that any stray cat or dog might have peed on it. Pina replied instantly: "We ate it always in Italy, don't you remember?" To which Almerinda snapped: "That was *cicoria,* not this—" Pina saw no practical difference, and so proceeded unhindered by her mother's comments, even loading her basket up higher with the bitter greens.

Their house was similar to the majority of houses in this section of east Pittsburgh. Almerinda kept everything about it, inside and out, tidy; Pietro had painted its metal porch awning red and green. The air around it on summer weekends was spiced by the hearty scents of tomato sauce, anise, and cigars. Pietro had proclaimed, during their first year in the house, that it was drafty in winter and baked like an oven in summer. He also cursed all the little things that needed fixing: cabinet doors that stayed ajar, dangling light fixtures, banging radiators. Some tasks he set his sons to finishing; others he entrusted only to himself, quietly enjoying the sudden opportunities to exercise his talent, regardless of what he said.

Pietro was, by trade, a shoemaker. Pina often repeated to her son, after Pietro was gone, that her father had made "a good shoe, not like today." Pietro consented to having made a good shoe, though he knew deep down that he had once made even better shoes. But, like so many things about his new world, those better shoes would have gone unnoticed. So he said nothing about his shoes, but threw his head back a bit, grimaced, and granted *"Eh!"* if anyone complimented them. That Pietro considered himself an artisan of the highest caliber was something only he knew, for he preferred not to accept compliments openly, and so eventually everyone stopped giving them. One thing they knew was that if Pietro fixed something it would never break again. What they didn't know was that he was never satisfied with what he did, and that nothing for him was ever completed until his grandfather's spirit had come to mark it so. It was a mark only Pietro could see, a mark of near perfection that was only evident on Sunday afternoons or early weekday mornings when the children were still asleep and Almerinda had preoccupied herself with setting the farina to boil.

Pietro's grandfather, Fiorentino Cavalieri, had also been an artisan. Young Pietro would watch him carefully as he bent hot iron into grillwork for the town's balconies, gates, and shop signs. Fiorentino had a long white beard, unkempt white hair, and narrow shining eyes. "You learn some trade, Pete. Be sure to, or next thing you know they'll be sending you to school. There's already such talk in the North. And whatever happens first in Piemonte will eventually make its way down to the Abruzzi. Listen! Pietro! Find out what your skill is and use it. Practice it. Make them see it before they take you and turn you into a modern imbecile." After such a little lecture the old Fiorentino would turn his lively eyes back onto his work, leaving Pietro free to hover like an angel about his shop, for Pietro did indeed feel like an angel in his grandfather's presence: gifted, fated, noted but unnoticed.

In 1880 Pietro turned fifteen. It was to be the most magical year of his life, the year a well ran dry inside him and he felt a lake filling up in its place; the year his childhood left but he was not yet sure of a thing called manhood; the year every sense of his was unlocked, and the world recreated itself daily before him. When he was well past his prime, and fraught with the problems that only the new country could bring, he sometimes looked back on that year, wanting to both relive and forget it, and able to do neither. For it was during that year that he arose at five o'clock to join two friends on an expedition to climb Mount Arazecca. Wearing his grandfather's hunting boots to protect his legs from the poisonous, ubiquitous *vipere* that populated his town, and carrying a knapsack filled with sausages, cheese, bread, and wine, he went to meet Pierluigi and Elio on the bridge at the edge of town: the clear water of the Sangro River broke like crystal over its rocks, as trout rose to the surface and flipped their tails into the cool air. When Pietro turned around to face the town he was leaving he saw it in an unfamiliar light; a pale silver that covered every cobblestone, window, chicken, roof tile, and tree. Only one lamp burned far up the old town hill, and he recognized the window it shone through. It belonged to his grandfather's house.

"Come on, Pete. Hurry! Hurry!"

He turned back and saw that the others had come, already anxious to find the path that led through the brown grass to the foot of Mount Arazecca. They thrashed through the lifting darkness as if being chased, and addressed one another sporadically and succinctly, as if learning a new way of speaking. Together they felt like reinventing everything that morning: the day was about to dawn for them, and they would direct its course, alone, on their manly expedition.

They saw no vipers, and only one wolfdog nursing her pups just beside the path after the sun had broken. She looked up at them, but didn't bark, and they passed by hurriedly, disregarding any consideration of pacing themselves during the five-hour climb.

The day's heat came gently as they began to cross the lower fields of sheep. A watchful shepherd or two waved at them from a distance, then they too grew small below, magically blending in with the still-life of a town whose activity they had known intimately from birth, though never all at once, until now. Young Pietro, his chestnut hair lifting from short gusts of wind, paused more than once to watch the shadows of clouds larger than Castel di Sangro approach, engulf, and then abandon the town.

In those days the railway to Castello had not yet been built, though markers had been laid halfway up the mountainside, past the sheep folds and viper line, where the first black locomotive would steam in from Roccaraso and Cinquemiglia, several years hence. Fiorentino had greeted the news of the impending railroad with caution. Soon, he'd said, they'd be sending in such nonsense as newspapers and city clothes to poison the character of Castello's young. Pietro and the others took pride in knowing that Mount Arazecca still belonged to them; and to the wild bears, rabbits, wolves, and deer of Abruzzo.

They reached the summit before noon, exhausted and hungry. In one direction lay Castel di Sangro, the first town in a line of towns that dotted the long valley. In every other direction lay the Apennine Mountains, and the dark green hills that made up this untamed part of Abruzzo. A stone pit there at the top contained the blackened ashes of many previous expeditions. The boys made their fire in it and held their sausages into it on long sticks. They ate them between thick slices of hard-crusted bread and washed them down with a communal bottle of Fiorentino's wine.

Pietro would have been content to take a siesta afterward, lying on the last shreds of green grass and watching hawks circle overhead; but Elio, as thin and agile as an Abruzzese deer, decided to climb the iron skeleton of a cross that townsmen had planted on the peak sometime before he or the others had been born. He reached its highest bar before Pietro had turned around, and there he sat, yelling "Screw you, Signor Toschi! Take your mangy old goat and give it to her up the ass..." Pierluigi, having finished the wine, fell back in raucous laughter, his generous stomach heaving. When he finished, the shimmering silence returned, but only for a moment. Pietro, who was only just beginning to close his eyes, straightened and sat up when he heard the thud. Elio had fallen from the cross.

At first, they could not see him, and thought he had rolled down the hill. But soon his disheveled black hair rose up, and stayed surprisingly still. Now Pietro knew all was not well; he tripped over rocks on his way to the foot of the cross. Elio looked up at him, serious but still light-headed from the wine, and said:

"I broke my goddam leg."

Pierluigi, having inherited a robust waistline from his mother's family, tired easily, and was of little use in helping Elio back down the summit. Pietro, on the other hand, was lean and sinewy: his muscles responded to any task at hand, and his family was known for their endurance during times of physical hardship. He carried Elio on his back three-quarters of the way down, until they met a farmer with his mule, which he lent to them on the condition that they return it in good condition, watered and fed.

When Pietro recounted this adventure to the old Fiorentino later, Fiorentino stopped briefly from his work, looked up, and said: "That jackass. Surely it was Giuseppe Andelucci. May his ancestors stay nailed in their coffins on Judgement Day."

These were the condemnations, the self-security and effortless wit, that made the adolescent Pietro ache to love his grandfather. If he could, he'd often thought, he would grow himself a long white beard too, and the more his grandmother would curse it and try to attack it with her shears, the longer he would let it grow. Why? "Just-so, that's all," as Fiorentino would have responded to those annoying little questions people ask one another about why they do what they do, live where they live, eat what they eat, or screw who they screw.

Fiorentino died the following year, when Pietro was sixteen. And Pietro didn't dare ask anyone why he had died, because he already knew the answer, in words that were painfully familiar to him: *Just-so, that's all.* It was a phrase his children, and their children, would hear often, though they would never know from where it came.

CHAPTER 2

PINA HAD MARRIED LATE BY HER FAMILY'S STANDARDS: thirty-four. She bore one son, who quickly replaced any affection she might have had for her husband. The boy's cousins knew that, by her, he could do no wrong. When he was killed in Korea, two years after the death of his father, Pina nearly gave herself up to God. She sat in the bedroom of her two-room apartment muttering curses to herself before finally going to bed, where visions of her past kept her in a state that was neither wakeful nor asleep, but in a certain limbo where there dwelled only pain. After a night of such horror, she would shuffle downstairs to the bathroom in her landlady's hallway, relieve herself, and throw water on her face. The wicked night then finally disappeared, and she would insist that there was still life in her, if only for the fact that she would someday see her grandchildren grow up.

She spoke of her grandchildren always to her friends in the neighborhood, but when pressed to offer details about them, her words almost always focused on the oldest, Manny, who often dropped by to see her, to have a cup of coffee, eat one of her Old World dinners, or listen to her tell stories as they studied the ancient photographs she kept neatly stacked in a brittle cardboard box. Pina would introduce him by saying: "Just like his father — look." And her old friends would smile and nod, seeing only a little resemblance. What they did see was that Manny laughed when his grandmother laughed, drew up his eyebrows when she did, smirked and frowned and bellowed out in ways that were familiar to them, because they were trademarks of Pina.

Manny too was not short of trademarks, things about him that everyone could see, even if he could not. Most often they were noticed by his wife, who early on tried diligently to search out and remove all those little spots on his shirts, or check to see that his tie wasn't too off-center, or remind him that his voice had risen thirty or forty decibels after his second glass of wine. Later she tried to think of these things as endearing, even if she couldn't completely ignore them. Somehow, they were the glue that kept the two of them together. This glue often spilled over into their living space, filling it with such sticky connective tissue as piles of magazines interlaced with newspapers and bills, clothes not dirty enough to be thrown into a hamper draped over chairs and doors, and congregations of food products lined up on the kitchen counter in anticipation of future dinner adventures.

San Francisco gave Manny great culinary comfort: he sampled and never tired of trying to reproduce dishes originating in Thailand, Portugal, Russia, Mexico, all parts of China, and of course from the native *cucina California*. Ellen was less adventurous in eating, as were their children, Josephine and Samuel, but that never deterred Manny from bringing home anything from dried lizard to canned shrimp paste. And he could always fall back on his grandmother's tomato sauce, which was a great hit with them all.

The year they moved West was the year Pina had died. Strangely, Manny felt less regret about moving so far away from his remaining family after she'd gone. Her death somehow signaled the death of Pittsburgh, or at least the Pittsburgh he had known. Ellen rolled her eyes once or twice at the idea of moving to San Francisco; she had never before been further than Ohio. But that look in Manny's eyes when he spoke of the job opportunities out there was a look she never wanted to go away. It represented the very thing she would never understand about him, the thing that made her love him. Privately, Manny was not sure it was best for them to move there, but that shred of uncertainty was exactly what made him want to do it.

During their first five or six years there they spoke of returning East someday, though nothing they did seemed to indicate that it might ever come true. Ellen was content with her work as a chemist at one of the large pharmaceutical companies, and Manny nearly lost himself daily in the cyberspace of his computers, both at work and at home. Always one of the first to try out new gadgets and software, he won a reputation at the office for quick mastery and originality in computer illustration.

They bought a house in North Berkeley, on a redwood hillside, two weeks before the birth of their second child. Then all talk of returning to Pittsburgh ceased, and Manny began thinking of himself as a pioneer of sorts: no one in his family had moved beyond western Pennsylvania.

In northern California the winters were something different—not snowy, nor bitter cold, nor endlessly gray. But they could chill you to the bone with their ruthless, dark rains. And people did get the flu. On one of those dark days, in early December, Manny stayed in his study all evening, unpacking and hooking up his new scanner. He was especially anxious to try out this more economical version of its big, expensive cousin at the office. In one distant corner of the study sat a sturdy old box filled with bits of memorabilia, old résumés, a few vintage news magazines, and an overstuffed manila envelope that had almost been reduced to felt. Inside it were Pina's old photographs.

Manny emptied the contents of the envelope onto his drawing desk and fished around for the smallest, most yellowed, tattered old photo in the pile. He settled on one he had never before focused on too closely, one in which Pina stood as a young woman next to her sisters, an aunt, and her brothers; while her father, mother, and two others stood behind them. He *presumed* it was her father there at the end of the back row: a one-eyed patriarch at the end of middle-age, what was left of his hair thrown back and uncombed, a cigar butt jutting up from his mouth. There was the hint of a smile in those long lips, and in the eye as well, though

Manny saw only the dark ring that outlined the spot where the other eye should have been: it had peeled away, a tear shorn from the surface of the yellowed print. It had carried one lapel with it, and then the base of a cock-eyed tie. This flaw made the old man even more enigmatic for Manny; he set on an immediate quest to restore Pietro Cavalieri, so that he might get a better glimpse of who he had been.

"Almerinda! Come here to have your beautiful face recorded for history. Pina! Maria! Everybody over here. NOW."

"Pete, what kind of nonsense are you up to now?"

"Bullshit."

"Pina!"

"What? That's what it is. And I don't want to do it. These plums are too good — I've already picked two hats full."

"Giuseppina. Don't make your father mad. He's already giving you the *malocchio*."

"You can give the picture to Giacomo, that nice fellow who's always knocking down our door..."

"Maria, shut up! Besides, I don't give a damn about him."

"She doesn't give a damn about her father. Holy Mother, how could I have borne this child?"

"No, *mamma*. She's talking about Giacomo, not *babbo*."

"Here we are then, Signor Purtelli. My beautiful family. See how beautiful they are! And all with their mother's, well, almost all — all right then. Take the picture. Take it, take it!"

"Mamma, Pina still has a plum in her mouth."

"And soon you'll have one up your ass!" Pina said.

He carried the scanned file on a disk in his pocket to work the next morning, tossing it onto a pile of other personal miscellanea, and nearly forgetting about it until he was ready to go home. But at 4:40 he saw the disk lying there, and quickly brought the file up

15

on his large office screen so that he could send it to their latest, photo-quality printer. The touching up he had done the night before showed more clearly now, although so did the flaws. The cloned right eye on his great-grandfather was not seamless; his lapel was much smoother than the gritty jacket surrounding it. Manny worked deftly with his computer tools, using this fresh new perspective to give more clarity to the reawakening photograph, reworking the cloned areas to perfection, removing creases and white specks, and further adjusting the density of grays. In the end he was still not satisfied (this photograph had become an obsession by now) and he finished it off by adding a sepia tint; this brought the figures to life.

It took nearly five minutes to travel the wires and process in the humming printer. By the time it had spit the image out Manny had shut down his machine, turned out most of the lights, and hung his leather bag from his shoulder. He took the print and carried it over to a long table for trimming; one drafting lamp hung over the table, the only light left.

Pietro Cavalieri looked up at him with two perfect eyes now; Pina stood leaning on her sister's shoulder, and she on her aunt's, who stood before her own sister, Almerinda. Together they produced a clear rhythmic motion, so clear now that Manny had to look again to be sure they hadn't moved. During the drive home he saw Pietro's face over and over again: he saw it in memories of his grandmother's face, in her brothers' faces, and a hint of it in photographs of his dead father. But it was more than a sum of features that compelled him to wonder; it was an expression, a glint of character that was familiar to him.

Before pulling in to his driveway he stopped at one of his favorite shoe stores. There he had once tried on a pair of soft, black, Italian shoes — the kind of shoes that do your feet honor during a long and thankless day. He wore the new shoes home, without feeling one bit of remorse for having spent $249 on them.

16

CHAPTER 3

PIETRO HAD SEEN SOMETHING LIKE A STREETCAR once before, in Naples. He had watched it turn into a deep alley and rattle away, as quickly as it had come, sending long sparks into the foggy dawn. He swore he would never ride in one. But in America they were everywhere, racing along the ground like hideous mechanical spiders while following their tightly-strung webs overhead. And the only way to get to where he was going, he was told, was to ride one. By his fourth day in that filthy new country he had been forced to break his promise.

There was one promise, though, that he would keep: he would not compromise his craft. Old Fiorentino must never be disappointed in him, no matter what evils he must endure to get by in this new *paese*. He carried his knife, his hammer, and his awl in a wooden box on his lap, holding it even more firmly every time the accursed electric car lunged him forward, or swung suddenly to one side. Pietro looked at no one; he counted the stops diligently as prescribed by his cousin Raimondo, waiting for the accursed city district where he was to get off and meet the shoemaker Falchi, Raimondo's employer.

The trolley passed through several neighborhoods, all of which looked similar to him: stout rows of tall brick homes built right up against one another, corner markets (with vegetables out in front), blackened stone schools, apothecaries, oily pigeons. Only the churches changed, representing other groups of Europeans that were utterly strange to him, for often they boarded the trolley when it stopped before their oddly shaped towers, with belfries either slanted or round, red or gold, single or double. The languages these broad-faced people spoke sounded like mad, hissing snakes, or nervous old hens. Their ancestors might have fought his in wars. It might even have been that their blood was cold, as it was rumored to be in those northern lands. They could

17

attack him now, and steal his box of fine, seasoned tools — his only possession.

"Grandpap," Pietro mused, "take these Germans away from us. Pray to the Almighty that we may live in peace among our own kind, without smelling those foul sausages on their breath." This entreaty left Pietro less vigilant in counting stops. The deepest part of the city appeared before him, growing larger and larger, but he felt neither diminished nor anxious, for he had old Fiorentino to keep him whole. A blur of windows and doors passed by, along with small groups of men in dark suits and gray hats. The car rattled over tracks that rose and fell unpredictably amid the smooth cobblestones. Pietro looked up and remembered where he was; a small round white sign with black-printed letters swayed from one of the lines overhead. It was another stop. Had he gone too far, not far enough? Were the Germans and Huns going as far as he? He had heard that having missed the central city stops, he would have to travel over a bridge and onto another foreign part of town, one filled with Russians, of all things. It would be better to get off before it was too late.

The car jolted once, and it began its slow glide again when Pietro rose. He called to the conductor: *Fermalo! Mi devo scendere,* unaware that the man could not understand him. But a young man near the front repeated his words, if not in his northern tongue then in American, so that the conductor put on the brakes and allowed Pietro to step down, holding his box tightly under one arm.

If he hadn't landed in that Russian part of town, then it must have been the Orient itself, because never had he seen so many pairs of dark, shifty eyes set into shady faces, not even in Napoli, which had been bastardized for centuries. Some of the men in dark suits milled about, it was true, but only to drop into one of the curtained restaurants. Walking up a low, endless hill, searching for the number written on his scrap of paper, Pietro smacked head-on into an African coming the other way. Now he knew he was in hell. What other infernal creatures could this city support?

"*Pietro! Vieni qua. Vieni, vieni!*"

Ah, a familiar phrase in a Godforsaken place. He recognized Raimondo immediately, and hurried off the road to shake his hand, then embrace.

"Pietro, we are waiting for you. This is Signor Falchi. He owns three shops on this street. First we'll have lunch, eh? There are many, many fine restaurants in this part of town. They are kept by the Lebanese."

"*Libanesi?*"

"*Arabi.*"

"*Arabi!*"

"Welcome to America, *cugino.*"

The sun, having exhausted itself before noon that day, never appeared for the remainder of it. The streetlight before Signor Falchi's shop flicked on, as soot rained down and cast an evil darkness over everything.

Pietro had seventeen pairs of shoes to repair. He held his third pair up to the shop light, as faithful now in his abilities as he had been in his ancestors' town, where he worked alone, and the sun was clear all day. At least he knew now that he had a place in this new life. The inferno could rage outside the window, but his hands would remain steady in their work. Something inside him must remain steady; something that was there not only for him but for his beloved Almerinda, and their children, as well.

CHAPTER 4

"WHAT? ANOTHER PAIR OF SHOES!"

Manny had been prepared for this.

"Manny—"

He had chosen, from among his many planned responses, to smile in her face and keep going on his merry way to the bedroom to change his clothes. He knew, just then, that she would go no further in her questioning. Some things were better left alone. He knew that deep down she had already realized he had a need for new shoes, that he was on a life-long quest to obtain the perfect pair.

When he returned to begin preparing dinner she addressed him in the same reticent tone:

"Manny—I like them."

She liked them! Was this a new ploy of hers, a subtle way of working up to something larger, perhaps a pledge by him that he would never buy more than, say, two pairs a month?

"Thank you."

If he'd gotten this far, he would test her no further. He went directly for the shitake mushrooms and plum sauce and staked out his territory on the counter to begin preparing dinner.

One hour later Manny cleared the table and loaded the dishwasher, while Ellen saw that the kids had done their homework and prepared for bed: their usual respective chores. Many things like this had been settled between them over the years—who picked out the children's clothes, who took them to the dentist, who cleaned up the vomit, who put the clean laundry away, who stayed up with the frightened puppy, who spoke up first when there was tension in the air. Manny played his part well; he knew he should, and he was absent-minded enough not to let any routine rob him completely of spontaneity.

This evening, however, he broke the routine by leaving a couple of pots on the stove, an empty glass on the table. And he did it deliberately, premeditatively, as if in adolescent defiance of community law. He sat down with his glass of wine and decided to buy a pair of boots the following day. When Ellen came back into the room it felt crowded. Too much about his life lately had been crowding in on him. He asked himself a hundred times a day, *Why? Why give in to this client? Why wear this costume to work every day? Why the house on a wooded hillside? Why the estranged neighbors, the predictable friends? Why Ellen?*

The last question was the clincher. When she touched his shoulder and said: "Are you all right?" he flinched, as if she had awakened him abruptly from a welcomed sleep.

"Yeah," he said. "I'm fine. Just daydreaming, you know."

She knew, because he spent about seventy-five percent of his life doing it.

"One of these days you're not going to come back to me," she said.

He looked up at her. She became the Ellen of All Ages: the Ellen he'd courted, the Ellen he'd married, the Ellen carrying their first child, worried Ellen, happy Ellen, morning Ellen, beautiful Ellen, absent Ellen. "What do you mean?"

She hit him on the back. "Nothing. Lighten up." Then she drew close to his face. "Everything's all right, isn't it?"

He returned a blank expression, complete with open mouth and frozen eyes: "Yeah, fine."

She walked away, but the impression her dark eyes and hair had made in the air lingered, like one of his thoughts. Was that the Ellen he loved, the elusive one? Or was it the tactile one, the one whose skin could make him lose contact with everything else, and draw him like silken quicksand into another world?

This was the problem. He preferred both. But it seemed that the elusive had become more enigmatic for him lately. Just about everything around him had become so. He had always thought of himself as invincible in some deep way. He could handle whatever came along and make the best of it. He had taken the initiative to move to California; they had secured jobs, started a family, bought a home. The whole thing now seemed like a film to him, one in which another Manny (and the elusive Ellen) had played the leading roles. But at this moment, with his latest new shoes soothing his tired feet like a lullaby, he felt as if he were imploding, and unable to stop it.

It was a feeling he was not happy to have.

Before the clock radio clicked on and rammed another day down his throat with its gruesome news report, Manny rolled over and opened his eyes. He had eight more minutes. So he closed them again.

There was something disturbing about waking up, though no less disturbing in falling back to sleep. In his dreams he had been entrusted to keep a secret, though the secret was lost to him. He spent days looking for it in old buildings, in places known to his past: the pediatrician's office, his first-grade classroom, the alley behind his mother's house, the room where he'd lost his virginity. He searched as if fulfilling a prophecy, though he wasn't sure who directed it, or what was expected of him. Some early elements of the dream had already disappeared, leaving him with a bone in his throat and a sense that nothing he could do that day would make it disappear.

Facing him late that morning was a desk that seemed to be eternally cluttered, a state of flux that somehow managed to remain static. He had his mini piles of impending jobs, jobs nearly completed, jobs nearly forgotten, and jobs too horrible to begin. He had his coffee-stained white mug, his miscellaneous stack (including semi-interesting mail), a trade magazine or two, and unopened boxes of software.

And in the other direction sat the screen, the human grit-stained keyboard, the computer with its host of troublesome peripheral devices, and a clean wall, which glowed in the environmentally friendly light like a portal to the anti-world.

Manny was early; he usually arrived at the office a good hour before anyone else. Not that he was such a dedicated worker; rather, he left early two days a week to pick up the children from school, and felt obliged to make up the time. Every day brought another schedule for Manny, and he followed each one diligently, like an athlete mastering an obstacle course. But this early morning hour gave him time to step into the sideline and recapture his dreams.

Some days, at this time, he spent ten or twenty minutes calling up his whims on the Internet. At first, he would be lost in it, then he would find a direction: a tour through the Slovak countryside maybe, or a catalogue of Chilean wines. And of course, there were always shoes: Italian shoes, English shoes, American shoes. Wholesale shoes and designer shoes, jogging shoes and relaxing shoes, boots, moccasins, and sandals. Some sites had pictures; others, only descriptions of shoes he could well imagine. But inevitably the next person would come into the office, then the next, and the next, and slowly the work day would begin.

On this morning, however, Manny did not feel the day beginning, no matter how many co-workers or clients walked through the door. He had relished the morning's dream too well; he had remembered that he was the keeper of its secret. He felt like doing something out of the ordinary: taking a long lunch maybe, or driving home later along a different route.

"Manny?"

"Manny?"

"Man-li-o?"

After a short lapse Manny looked up from his screen. It was Linda, the newcomer at the office — younger than Manny by a few years, but already playing a role that was becoming distasteful to him.

"Yes, Linda."

"I'd like to talk to you about scheduling a seminar."

"Scheduling a seminar? For what?"

"It's something I think we ought to do to help our clients become more computer literate, as well as bring in new clients."

"Did you talk with Henry about this?"

"Screw Henry. He never listens to us anyway."

"But he's our boss."

"So."

"So, so…" he trailed off into something unintelligible to both of them. He could see the two of them with their tray of slides, pointers, and computer manuals inflicting suffering on otherwise happy clients during their golden lunch break. The vision made his hair stand up.

"I don't know if they'll go for it."

"They will," she stated. "I've already spoken with some of them. A lot of them feel intimidated when they come here; at least we can help them…"

Her words became a foreign language; her body turned translucent, like a reflection in glass. Manny began deconstructing her face, seeing each feature separately, and wondering what they added to the whole Linda. Did her eyes tell a different story than her mouth? Her forehead from her chin? He began thinking about the others in the office, their hodgepodge faces of disunity, the different stories that came from each particular part of the face. What was she telling him now? Was it really about the office, or was it something about her?

"…you know what I mean, Manny?"

"No."

"What do you mean, no?"

"I mean I didn't hear you, and I'd rather not talk about it now."

"Oh."

He wasn't sure whether she was miffed, or just being her own succinct self, as she turned to go away, growing back to opacity under the harsh light beyond his cubicle.

Chapter 5

GIUSEPPINA NEVER WANTED TO GO BACK TO ITALY, not even to visit her mother's cousins. In her mid-twenties, she saw the people there as imprisoned by needless toil and unbending tradition. Why wash clothes on a rock by the river when she could put them in a washing machine, which was now all the rage? And why marry, if she didn't want to? Why not go to work every day, and be a real part of America? She rarely restrained herself in voicing these opinions; often they landed right between Pietro's eyes, setting him off like a firecracker:

"What? And you'd be happy enough never to visit your ancestors' graves again, I suppose?"

"Right. All they're seeing now is potatoes, anyway."

"Pina! Your grandfather is listening to you this moment. He gave you your life! Have respect for him!"

"What? I remember him on All Soul's Day—and just as well as though I were at his grave."

By now Pietro would have risen from his seat and thrown his hands up. Pina would not back away, only set her mouth and raise her chin just long enough to sustain her point before moving on to another one. This bartering might have gone on endlessly if it hadn't been for Pietro's lack of patience, especially when the subject of family respect was in question.

As a child Pina rarely did as she was told. She had an answer or an argument for everything, and often they were very good ones. Having one leg a few centimeters shorter than the other, she was exempt from many of the household chores; she even went to school and learned to read, more at the urging of Almerinda than Pietro, who remembered what Grandpap Fiorentino had said about that modern institution. There were only ten children in her class, and every one of them wore better clothes than Pina, and had better speech, and brought in gifts for the teacher, and had fathers who believed in the virtue of their schooling. Pina, however, rarely missed an answer, picked up new words quickly, and did her homework without anyone's insistence. In her flashing eyes the mature teacher saw vitality, curiosity, transcendence. But these were the qualities that made Pietro both love and fear her, for they were the qualities that made him love and fear himself.

If anyone asked how his children were, Pietro would answer, "They're alive, thank God." But when pressed he would always mention his oldest, Pina, who had the quickest wit of them all, and who received only the highest marks at school (though he wasn't sure what those marks meant). He would quickly add that she knew everything there was to know about his craft, and if God had intended women to be shoemakers, she would have made a fine one.

Once, in a fury of passion, Pina stole into her father's shop during siesta to measure out the leather for a set of shoes that she herself intended to make. She was ten years old. The shoes were to be for Ippolita, the old widow of Via Arazecca, who swore more than anyone Pina had ever known, and who went barefoot, even in winter, because she had no money for shoes. Just as Pina had cut the last piece from scraps she'd found lying in the floor she heard the beaded fly netting hanging at the shop's entrance rustle, having been pushed aside by her father's great hand. He saw her at once, and she knew from his long pause that he would show no mercy.

"What are you doing? What's that in your hand?" He spoke without inflection.

"Nothing."

"Don't lie!"

"Nothing!"

He called her name, not her full name as slowly and deliberately as her mother did, but those two syllables loud and clear and short, like a hawk's cry.

She froze, then caught her breath:

"I was just cleaning up for you, *Babbo*. I thought you'd like coming back from siesta to a clean shop…"

"I like my shop the way it is. I know where all my tools are, and how much leather is in each pile. Who put you up to this? Your mother?"

She didn't answer.

"Tell me!"

"No! No one did. I don't know why you have to get so —"

"Don't talk back to me!"

She threw down the leather and ran past him, feeling his great stillness while she moved. But it would not deter her from coming back the next day, and finding what she needed in those inconspicuous piles of scrap.

Pietro tried to soothe himself by saying a Hail Mary, but when that didn't work, he turned viciously onto his work, producing shoes that were fine enough to dream about. Weeks hence, on a cool, cloudy day, he passed Ippolita Signorile on the street, and noted the roughly-hewn shoes she wore, sewn together by his very own brown thread! In an instant he knew how she had gotten them, and after having bade her good day he turned to hurry back home, feeling the thickness of his heavy belt. But a hail from an old friend broke his spell, and he ended up taking coffee instead, with a faraway look in his eyes as they sagged and lost their intensity. Something left his blood and gathered in his heart, which smoldered and warmed over with pride for his daughter.

He too had been ten years old once. Having endured enough adult babbling, led by his father, about the final stages of the *Risorgimento*, state-run education, and taxes, he lit out one spring afternoon for the Sangro river. There he would be able to corner trout in small pools and stone them to death. He had oiled his boots up well to repel the water and snakes.

The evening was young, and the sun tilting over Mount Arazecca enough to brighten the undersides of trembling poplar leaves and changing facets of the clear river water. Young Pietro stopped, surrounded by this flashing silver light, and gazed ahead, where the narrow river turned into a grove of darker trees. There, playing in the water fully clothed in his costume of thunderous colors, was a Gypsy boy, who was not older than Pietro himself. Pietro watched him for some time before taking another step. He was sure the boy would call up every evil spirit imaginable and bring doom upon Pietro's family if he was discovered. He knew a lot about Gypsies, though he had never spoken with one. "They practice witchcraft," Nonno Fiorentino had advised him, "and will stop at nothing to get what they want."

If the boy hadn't noticed him yet he could turn and run away along the riverbank, and any evil spell that had been cast upon him would be broken...

"Hey, you!"

Pietro froze, his back to the boy.

"Come here!"

"I won't!"

"You don't want to see the biggest fish ever to swim in the Sangro?"

"I don't speak to liars."

"How do you know I'm lying?"

"Because I myself caught the biggest fish in the river here just last week."

"But this is his brother, and he is really beautiful, with a nice pink belly and green and gold spots all over him."

"Really?"

"Come and see him, quickly, before he gets away!"

Pietro took two steps in the water, then made his way along the dry riverbank to the shaded spot where the boy stood. They regarded one another furtively, never eye-to-eye.

The boy's skin was the color of dark hazelnuts, unlike the olive-toned skin of Pietro's family, and of most of the families of Castello. His eyes were blacker than any Arab's or Sardinian's (for Pietro had heard that such eyes existed in those exotic lands). He wore a red, silken vest and dark green pantaloons, cinched with a blue sash. He kicked a few more stones around the little pool he had made near the bank, and Pietro saw that his feet were bare.

"Don't you know this place is crawling with vipers?"

"*Vipere?*" the boy answered, "I'll bet you'll never see one here again. My grandmother cursed them all away last spring."

"You're a real liar." Pietro looked into the water. "And where's that fish you were talking about anyway?"

"Santa Maria!" said the Gypsy. "He's gone."

"And just as certain he was never here," said Pietro. "You're nothing but a lying Gypsy!"

The boy ran off, splashing through the trickling water like a startled deer. Pietro lifted his left foot and saw that he had been standing on a viper, its head smashed but tail still twitching.

"Ah-hah!" Pietro shouted. "You'll never beat me!" But then he saw that another had crawled onto his other boot, and a third had just peeped over a round rock behind him. He flew home faster than a hawk, shaking his feet in the air with every light step, a cold shiver traveling down his spine.

CHAPTER 6

JOSEPHINE CAME DOWN ON SATURDAY MORNING wearing an outfit she had picked out for her twelfth birthday: a velvety dark blue sweater out at the waist and black tight-fitting pants. As Manny sipped his morning coffee at the kitchen table he looked up and saw that she had entered that fragile space between girl and young woman. She said nothing to him on her way to the refrigerator for a glass of milk (she'd heard it was good for her complexion), drank it quickly, and skipped out of the room like a six-year-old.

Manny was left still thirty-eight, presbyopic and graying, with his cup of increasingly bitter coffee.

"Dad! Let's go!" Jo called from the foyer.

"I'm finishing my coffee."

He found a pen on the table and began making sketches on the back of a junk mail envelope: a solution for the pet food company logo he'd been working on. Within seconds he had lost contact with the rest of the material world; just as the answer was about to present itself Jo's footsteps on the cold tile floor reawakened him.

"Daddy, will you *come on?* I'm *not* going to be late again."

"Shhh! I'm thinking."

He felt her gaze searing into his back, but held on defiantly to his advancing idea. Finally she let out a howl that succeeded in breaking his concentration for good.

"All right. Thanks for ruining my idea."

"But we're late!"

"I'll write them a note."

"Daddy, I'm not in second grade anymore. They don't want notes. They want me to be on time! Ohhh—I can't wait til I can drive. Then I won't have to wait for *anyone.* And you can have all the stupid ideas—"

"Stop it! We'll go when I'm ready, and that's that."

He saw that little shake he had given her, exactly like the one she'd had when she was seven or eight years old, after refusing for the fifth time to finish her roast beef, until the headache that had been brewing in him all day finally overflowed, and he let it out in her direction.

They drove off that morning in their usual silence, though this silence carried something else with it: a new fear, or uncertainty, of the future. How would all other morning rides with her father be? What would he have to talk about with her now, knowing the old admonitions and reminders would sound hollow, and insensitive? He stole a glance at her, and saw the same uneven part line of her hair, the same empty (or was it awestruck?) expression on her maturing face. What about her might be changing, and what remain unchanged?

She left the car not looking at him until after she'd closed the door again. Then he saw her smile quickly and silently through the window, her brown hair falling over her cheeks, and eyes firmly attached first to his, then away in the direction of her waiting friends. It seemed that he had only blinked, and she was gone.

Amid the pile of unopened mail at the office that morning was a brochure announcing the annual graphic designers' convention. It was to be held in Pittsburgh.

Manny noted the date, then headed for the coffee pot, still empty at this hour. While dumping the premeasured grinds into the filter holder he looked out the tall, tinted window to an awakening, wintry San Francisco day. Grayish clouds fell obliquely through the sky, electric buses sent sparks into the air, and tidy new buildings gleamed softly, while the concrete planters surrounding them still held green.

His reflection stuck in the window, translucent, holding an empty cup, as snow fell onto his back and through his hair, moistened his upper lip and eyelashes. It swirled like smoke in little eddies before him, fell from the boughs of weighted pine trees, and coated his boyhood world with a firm, clean magic. The magic stayed as long as the snow did, as long as it fell all around him and filled up his footprints and sledding tracks. In it he was neither cold nor tired nor timid, and he lived in this temporary, suspended state until his mother called him in.

"Manny? Is the coffee ready?"

No answer.

"Hello? Is anyone in there?"

The warm winter world of California came flooding over him, and he felt a small chill run through him. For the California office air, as it hit his skin, was not warm, but cold.

Linda poured the fresh coffee, and continued her conversation:

"Did you hear where the annual GDA meeting is this year?"

"Yes, In—"

"Pittsburgh! How *gross!* Do you think anyone will go?"

"I'm going."

"Really? Why?"

"That's where I come from. It's really not a bad place. And hey, the air's cleaner there than it is here. Where did you grow up?"

"In The Richmond."

"And you never went anywhere else?"

"Why should I?"

With that closure to the topic she darted off in the direction of her ringing phone, leaving Manny feeling more defensive than he ever had about his home town. By the end of the day Linda had coached just about everyone in the office in providing Manny with friendly jeers about his birthplace, which he took good-naturedly, but half-heartedly. He had, for the first time they could remember, nothing to say in return. Though a lot of thought did swell up in him that day. He found himself becoming more and more anxious, with no idea of how to release it.

Driving home over the Bay Bridge that evening he felt that chill again — as though it had blown right through the car and under his clothes. Another nasty West coast flu brewing? Or something calling from another world? By the end of the bridge he had forgotten it: he glided down the stilted ramp onto the highway, bound north, to his family and home.

Sam was the first to whirl by him after Manny had opened the door. He barely stopped, on the return run, long enough to render his latest list of things to be had next Christmas, eleven months away. Manny studied the very serious look on his son's face, until it slipped away with a smile when Manny interrupted by lifting him into the air.

"Hey! Put me down!"

"Nope!"

"Put me down, put me down, put me down —" he broke into a long giggle, which stopped only when Jo stomped by on her way to see her mother about something that must have been unbearably important.

Manny heard their voices coming from the kitchen:

"I *told* you not to put it in the dryer. Don't you listen?"

"Don't use that tone of voice with me. I forgot. It's as simple as that."

"Yeah, right."

"Manny!"

Now the day drained out of him; there was nothing left but a vacuum to be filled by the hard edges of words.

"Manny, will you come here please?" Ellen's tone was both commanding and conciliatory. She was about to call again, this time louder, when he stepped into the kitchen.

"Hi Jo."

"Hi." She remained smileless, looking down. Ellen would have started right in, but Jo lifted her head and fired:

"*She* ruined my favorite sweater. And it was the last one they had. I think she should have to buy me a new one."

"But you said it was the last—"

"Ohhh! Daddy! You don't get it. I need a *new* one. It doesn't have to be exactly like the other one."

Ellen looked at him.

"It was an accident. She just throws her clothes all into one big pile, and there it was like everything else."

"Did you ever hear of reading the tag?" Jo put in.

"That's it." Ellen blew. "Forget getting a new sweater with that tone of voice. I'll remember this next time you do something by accident. You can be sure I will."

"Ohhh! She's so mean!"

"And if you'd do your own laundry this never would have happened."

"I don't have time to do…" Jo called back as she trotted up to her room to slam the door.

Manny had not taken another step since he'd entered the room. Ellen threw up her hands and shook her head:

"She's incredible. She leaves her things lying everywhere and expects everyone else to pick them up." She paused. "Just like you."

Manny ignored her searing gaze.

"Maybe—" he returned.

"What?"

"You're not the neatest thing to hit the world either, you know. She could have gotten it from you too."

"Manlio Salvatore Cavalieri."

"What?"

"You're ridiculous. I have to run to the bathroom. Watch this steak."

There were some things she just didn't have a clue about. Who would make a streak under the broiler instead of out on the grill?

"I decided to make it inside," she echoed back to him from the hallway, "because it's chilly today."

He wondered how she had come to believe (like the natives) that fifty-eight degrees was chilly, but knew there would be no use in entering that territory with her. He never knew how much of her acclimation was real, and how much an affectation. Under the circumstances it was best just to proceed with the ruined steak, and hope the air would soon change.

CHAPTER 7

ON SHIPS THERE IS TIME TO THINK. On trains there is a destination to watch out for; passengers enter and leave your coach. The train slows and may come to a standstill for no apparent reason. If you fall asleep you may miss your stop. If you can't pay the fare they might tell you to get off. But on a ship there is one destination; everyone is heading there, and no one will disembark unless you are disembarking too. Until that time, confusion gives way to rest. Life is suspended. You are in between lives, carried by Mother Earth in a gently rocking cradle to a new birth.

Pina would not sleep on the ship, at least not for the first forty-eight hours: there was too much to see, too much that was new. She relished the newness, the new life that was coming. Almerinda, along with Pina's sisters, did not welcome the new. They dwelled on their fear until it welled up inside them and made them seasick. They remained on the edge of fear and sickness every day during the two-week trip.

Pietro was not afraid; nor was he sick, or excited. Pietro sat on the bench in the crowded cabin, or strolled the slippery deck, and thought. It was the only time in his life that he could do nothing but think.

At first he relished the sun, and the freedom of riding in limbo: unable to carry out his new responsibilities yet in America, and playing no part in directing the affairs of the ship, Pietro took the ride as a little vacation — probably the only one he would ever know. The thinking came easy to him, though he was able to do it only after Almerinda herself had scolded him for moving nervously about the cabin and deck, "like a cock at dawn." "Go upstairs and sit," she determined, "and don't come back until you've had enough of it." Naturally, the first thing he thought of up there was her. They hadn't made love in three weeks, which by now seemed unendurable to him. If America didn't come soon he'd take her out of that smelly, overcrowded shit-hole of a cabin and heave her onto the deck, under the stars, yes, just as if they were young. And he would sing out if he wanted to, why not, and kiss her from head to foot. He still felt that way about her; he still saw those young, flittering blue-gray eyes of hers under the stern shape of her middle-aged face. He remembered the bat that had flown into their room on their wedding night: the terror in her eyes, and the laughter that overcame them as he chased it out. And how they settled again, unsettled about what the night would bring....

A wave came rolling into the hull of the ship, sending up a light spray that reached Pietro's face. As it lifted, a veil was torn from his past, leaving other scenes to dwell on, other impulses that surfaced as he tried to locate his feelings in the abyss through which he was sailing. He wondered how he could have worked so hard in Castello, forgetting the trout-filled river, the sapphire sky and pine woods of the foothills. They were as distant to him now as America. He wanted to forget them, but he couldn't. He could smell the rosemary and acacia after rain, the light smoke from burning hearths in winter, the pork sauce Almerinda had made for dinner. He had never allowed himself to love these things, because he never had time to think of anything but work, about feeding his family, about whether or not anyone would want to buy a pair of shoes that week. And now he found himself, alone, sitting on the deck of a cold ship, thinking.

Might he have gone to school, like Pina, if he had been born in her time? Might he have learned to read those damned newspapers too? And add large numbers in his head? How could he blame Pina for wanting to learn these things? Why did he never tell her he envied her for it? Or that he was proud of her? He could not tell her now, not now as they sailed to a new land, a land heavy with new responsibilities and uncertainties for all of them. There would be no time for praise, no time for thinking, no time for anything but making a living, and making a living that was better than the one he'd tried to make in Castello. He had to do this, because if he failed, he would bring shame upon himself, his family, and all their ancestors.

Pietro closed his eyes. The stars of the open sea sky had imprinted themselves on the backs of his eyelids, each glowing faintly red on a black background. He had not looked at the stars so intently since he was a boy; now they were imprinted on his eyes, the eyes of Pietro Cavalieri of Castel di Sangro, eyes as plain and common as anyone's. What would he do with them there? They did not fit him, it seemed; and yet they drew him back to childhood, and forward to a new life on another side of the spinning world.

Pina did not have time to think on that floating town; there was so much that demanded her attention, her action. She could spend twenty minutes studying the waves crashing against the bow of the ship, not thinking, but studying. She could follow one of the ship's mates in his dark uniform and stop abruptly if he turned his head, or listen to the boy from Ateleta play songs he had written himself on his Spanish guitar. One thing she would not do was listen to her mother and sisters talk about all the troubles they would soon be facing, or how they would miss the sunsets of Mount Arazecca.

"I don't give a damn about those sunsets," Pina said. "And besides, I've heard they're much more beautiful in America."

"*America,*" Almerinda said in her softly outspoken way, "*America.*"

Pina would not hear these laments in the face of the beautiful open sea. Wherever it took her would be better than the landlocked valley of Castello, with its landlocked minds and hearts. Maybe she would take long walks through the big American city, looking at the faces of those who came from all over the world, wondering what they were thinking, where they were going, how they too had been unlocked from old ways of thinking. For Pina the world was spinning fresh, and taking her with it. She would have it no other way.

American trains were vicious and gentle at the same time: sure of their direction, smoothly gliding, and stopping only where they were supposed to stop. They could coast along a hot plain and then ease through the cool foothills of the mountains, without causing Almerinda to wonder whether it was strong enough to pass through, as she had wondered while riding the crowded train through the Abruzzese Apennines.

She had already resigned herself to this new life, whatever it may bring—serious faces, strange trees, endless tracks that carried them through dark tunnels and over wide rivers. It seemed America was endless, that it might suck the life out of you and spit you back into those deep forests, and no one would notice. It seemed to her as she closed her eyes that that train could go on forever, even after they'd gotten off, carrying millions of others to its mysterious destination.

Her Pietro was finally asleep beside her, even leaning into her arm, knowing that she needed to feel him, to keep her memories of Castello alive. She could not remember the last time he had fallen asleep beside her like this. This would be her only time to to think, against her grain, about herself.

She remembered a little song her grandmother had taught her one snowy evening, when the world had been confined to an Abruzzese valley and its people, living and dead. The song had taken away new fears that were creeping up on her, a ten-year-old, as she approached the end of her childhood —

Dai, Mariuccia, là.
Il mondo ti lascerà.

Vieni a casa, a casa non stai
altro che ne penserai.

Almerinda blessed herself and kissed her fingers, begging forgiveness of her ancestors for leaving them, for breaking an oath that ran in her blood. For who had ever left Castel di Sangro, whose very name sealed this oath, and bore testimony to each generation of the faithfulness of time? Where would they bury Almerinda, Pietro, and their children, and what spirits would keep them company there? At last now, while riding through a darkened tunnel under a Pennsylvania mountain, she allowed herself to drop a tear. It fell onto Pietro's cheek, and he instinctively raised his hand to her face.

CHAPTER 8

MANNY BOUGHT THREE NEW PAIRS OF SHOES for his trip. Before leaving he showed one of them to Ellen, who chose to ignore the act completely and instead planted a very sensuous kiss on his lips, as if to say *This is more important than shoes.* Jo, however, had found the other two pairs under her parents' bed the night before (she had been looking for a pair of hers) and coolly remarked that they were nice, though a little *stiff.* Manny concluded that stiff was not an acceptable category for contemporary shoes to be in — they should look worn before you buy them.

This is what he thought about on the flight to Pittsburgh: worn shoes. It seemed that he was always looking for the perfect new pair of shoes, and yet he wanted them to fit him so well that it would seem he'd worn them all his life.

When the plane touched down Manny woke up, surprised to feel contact with the earth again. He had felt at home with the clouds, belonging both nowhere and everywhere at once. And Pittsburgh, where he had grown up, awakened nothing inside him. It was as if all his memories had been buried in those clouds. He was left with an unmitigated present, in a city that no longer belonged to him.

It was a good feeling.

During the taxi ride to his downtown hotel, at dusk, he let himself empty of any expectation he'd had about this conference. He let himself fill up with everything that was new, even if that meant denying his past. The dark green hills that hedged in the highway could have been the hills of Bavaria or Peru; the tunnel could have run under the San Francisco Bay. The glittering lights on the water might have been burning angels, denying the element. The city itself might have come from another time, someone else's life.

The hotel was full of unfamiliar faces, faces from all corners of the country, all moving without direction, creating petty conversation, creating the first act of the convention play. He had to leave.

The night was still heavy with the scent of midsummer heat, a scent that drew Manny along with it, welcoming him in a way the grand hotel couldn't. He walked in the direction of the old Strip District, past the restored train station and crossroads that led to several bridges over the Allegheny River. When he was young the bridges had been black; the stone block of the train station and county jail likewise had shown black. The black grime of industry had paved the streets and streaked every brick building. You could feel it on your face and smell it on your clothes.

All that had vanished in the years he'd been gone, and Manny only now saw the result of the transformation, a transformation that had allowed the city's buried colors and smells to surface, like a liberated culture. The longer he walked, the more he noticed: the glass-bound cafés with their clientele on display, rollerbladers gliding by, career men and women obtaining their cars after a long day of work, a small abandoned church; and then, slowly, the food shops that announced the beginning of the Strip.

It was here that time began to unravel for Manny; he saw fresh pasta hanging behind windows, smelled shellfish and fruit, saw baskets of cut flowers pushed up against a curb, smelled Mediterranean cheeses, and heard old voices, voices that had been tucked away in the folds of his memory.

"*Quanto ci viene?*"

"*Cinquanta.*"

"*Che disgrazia! Meno, mi sembra.*"

The fruits and vegetables kept their oranges, yellows, reds, and greens, but the sky had lost all clarity, and the figures moving near him were clad in shadowy grays and black.

In their faces were worries that were less familiar to him, marks of pain or grieving that this country no longer afforded. They spoke a dozen languages, carried cloth bags with fresh whole chickens and wrapped fish popping out of them. Children passed him by without looking up.

Quickly, then, even the curbside flowers lost their color; the sky turned into a charcoal gray, and only the pale faces of these darkly clad people showed above a world of grays. Past the vegetable stands stood a small line of shoe stalls: in these, men bowed over black shoes that had lost their sheen, restitching and replacing old soles or heels. In one of these stalls Pietro Cavalieri sat too, boldly polishing the pair of work boots he had just restored. He did not look up, nor even take note of Manny, who cast a distant look on him from where he stood outside the entrance.

Chapter 9

MANNY'S FEET SLIPPED IN AND OUT OF HIS SUEDE shoes as the keynote speaker drew another polite response to a lukewarm joke. This time Manny did not laugh; he took another look at an interesting face (across the row) and then back to the designs in the dimmed ceiling.

Now every now and then a client comes to you with...

Shoes. He needs another pair of shoes. These are killing his heels, and there's no time to break them in. The interesting face belongs to a woman. About forty-five. No, younger? The woman is not Ellen. Everything here is not Ellen, is not his life. It is something new and old: the history of his life, and what will become of it.

You can't imagine what they're thinking when they say you haven't...

During his walk last night he saw them: the dead, the living face of his past. A past rooted in his bones, known and unknown to him. He felt comfortable there, among them, where everything had already been decided—lives lived, well-defined and full of urgency, survival. They did not look at him, but he knew they could see through him: they knew that his life was not like theirs. He had come further in some ways. In others he had fallen behind.

Theirs was an Old World order, an order that expressed itself in the color of their clothes, the line of their lips, hand gestures and embraces. Nothing was mistaken, nothing taken for granted. Manny's world, on the other hand, had to be reinvented daily— sometimes with poetically inspired results, but more often with a heart, back, head, and neck ache. And because everyone else in Manny's world was also reinventing it, no two people could ever live in quite the same world. Spouses included.

The Old World was attracting him. In it, problems were definable, and everyone must have agreed on what they were. How nice it must be to all be suffering together, engaged in the same battles, against disease, poor wine, and mothers-in-law!

Now what if the attractive woman across the aisle were part of that Old World? Would she be sitting there, listening so attentively, or not be there at all, but fulfilling a role less commercial, more domestic? Manny got a good look at her now; she looked as bored as he was. That blank stare of hers appealed to him. It told him that she too must have better things on her mind, that she had not been duped into careerism after all.

He could not describe her style, or even determine whether or not she had any. Her hair, a dark and dull brown, seemed to grow naturally away from her face and down to her shoulders, requiring no time at the beauty parlor, or even at her dressing mirror. Her profile was pointed yet relaxed; her lips reserved yet capable and ready for any challenging discourse. Her head tilted back slightly, showing that she pretended to listen but also that she was a little tired. Manny liked the simple nature of her dress: a small, indiscernible print of pastels on a dark blue background. Might she be French, or South American?

The room emptied into applause, and the startling event made Manny realize he was staring at her, and made her realize that someone was staring at her. She turned to face him so quickly he hadn't time to gather his wits. And there they were: two full brown eyes — intelligent, thoughtful, and wary — on a face as calm and resolute as the Moon's.

CHAPTER 10

IT WAS A DAY FOR PICKING PLUMS. The Purtelli family had invited Pietro and his family to their home in Vandergrift—a home that had been theirs already for two generations. Nonno Purtelli had arrived in America just as Nonno Fiorentino Cavalieri had been cursing it to Pietro. And now Giancarlo Purtelli, a grandson of the immigrant, had established himself as the head of a small bricklaying company. He used his house and orchard as a welcoming ground for the newly arrived, pouring them wine made from his own grapes, and serving them *spaghetti all chitarra* made by his mother and Mexican wife.

Almerinda's inclination was to head straight to the kitchen to help them, and it was considered right that she do so by the Purtelli women, but Giancarlo, as always, stepped in to announce that none of his guests should ever lift a finger unless it be for picking fruit. And that included the women. So he led them all up the knoll to the spot where seven plum trees glowed purple and green under the midday sun.

Plums had not been plentiful in Castello, and Almerinda frowned when she bit into one. Giancarlo took it from her hand and threw it on the ground. "Here," he said, reaching for another. "This one is sweet." Almerinda then interviewed every plum she picked, comparing its size, weight, and color to the good one she had just eaten. Her daughter Maria did the same, placing only every fourth or fifth one into her basket. Angelo and Martino, Pina's brothers, stopped picking and began throwing plums at one another and the others, including the Cavalieri cousins who had come along that day. But Pietro and Pina kept on picking their plums radically, grabbing two or three at once, never checking for insect holes or firmness, and eating any big one that caught their eyes.

The baskets filled, and the sun grew hot. Almerinda rested on an old stump in the shade of a maple tree. Pietro lost himself among its cool, leafy branches. Pina and her sisters compared their catches, and the boys were about to show off theirs when Giancarlo's son, thirteen-year-old Luca, came running up the hill as if ready to announce something important.

"We're going to take a picture!" he shouted. "Come on, everyone! My dad says to stand over here..."

"*Cos'ha detto?*" Almerinda put to her husband. *What did he say?*

"It's a photographing machine," he said.

"Oh no," she said. "I'm scared of that."

"Now what? What's the matter with you?"

"Hey. Don't you remember what happened to Signora Ferrucci back in Castello? She died within one week after they took her picture. They say a *mal'anima* lives in that box, and—"

"*Basta!*" Pietro shouted. *Enough!* "Come on, everyone. Under that big tree over there."

Almerinda slowly made her way to the great oak, crossing herself several times along the way. "It's true," she whispered to Pina, who looked askance and pretended not to hear.

Giancarlo Purtelli himself arranged everyone according to age, with Pietro and Almerinda in the background (along with Pietro's cousin and his wife), Pina and others of her age in the middle, and children in the foreground. Everyone but Almerinda could not help smiling, and half of the mouths were chewing plums when Giancarlo finally gave the signal. At that point Pina raised a plum in front of her, and nearly everyone followed suit.

"*Bello.* Giancarlo said. "*Bravissimi!*"

CHAPTER 11

PINA BEGAN SHRINKING WHEN SHE WAS forty-four, starting from her height of four feet ten inches and ending up, in her later years, at four-six. When she came to Manny's house during his childhood she would say to him: "Next time you pass me up." And sure enough, when Manny was only ten, he did.

From then on Manny began to notice that they were always, in some way, on the same level. At family gatherings he would notice her sitting in her usual cross-legged style, with arms folded over a wide belly and feet just barely touching the floor, obviously thinking of anything other than what the other adults were talking about. At first he'd thought it was her inability to communicate very well in their language. Then, at around age sixteen, he began to recognize that she was bored, and much better amused by her own thoughts than by anyone else's. This was something Manny could relate to, especially in early adolescence.

Manny grew more and more curious about her family. Once, after he had learned how to drive and made a visit to her small apartment in the Italian neighborhood of town, he said, "Nonna, what was my grandfather like?"

"Jim?" she replied.

"Yeah."

Her face contorted into a look of surprise, wonder, and disdain. Then she waved one hand in the air and uttered a long, Italian "Ehhhhh," which ended in such a staccato note that Manny knew he was treading on unwelcome territory. But after a long pause, during which Manny tried to change the subject, she interjected: "Some-a time he bring me coffee in bed, too." Manny decided he would have to find out more from other relatives, Pina having had a more or less biased opinion of his grandfather from the start.

He found that Jim had been a gentle, but firm man who had opinions but never forced them on others, except his son. Manny wondered whether his father would have been the same way with him, and whether his own personality might have developed differently had he lived.

"Now your father," Manny continued with Pina. "What was his name?"

"Pete."

"What?"

"Pete. *Pietro* in Italian."

"And your mother?"

"What? What for you want to know?"

"I don't know. I just do."

"*Almerinda.*"

Manny looked up from the kitchen table at the sound of her name. "That's beautiful. Was she beautiful?"

"My mother? In Castel di Sangro, my country, everybody says she's the most beautiful. No like me. I look-a like my father."

Pina laughed, drawing Manny with her, until they both lost their breath and forgot what they had been talking about.

"Nonna. Hey, how do you like my new shoes?"

She regarded them carefully, as if she knew something about shoes that he didn't.

"Well, not so bad, not so good. They no make a good shoe today, not like what my father make."

"Pietro?"

"That's right."

"He was a shoemaker?"

"That's right. And he make a good shoe. No like today."

Manny was surprised to learn that she had taken her father's craft to heart, and wondered what other things of that lost world were buried there. For a moment, while sitting in his grandmother's small kitchen waiting for her to prepare dinner, he wondered what it might be like to wander around in the past, in her past. But the aromas of pork-flavored tomato sauce and grated pecorino cheese brought him quickly back to the present, and, being a hungry sixteen-year-old, he stayed there with her, in the present, for quite a long time.

The painting class Manny found himself in was not small: seventy-five graphic artists crammed the room; along with a projector, an easel, a portable chalkboard, and the instructor. The room's walls curved along the sides, giving it a feeling of intimacy that was more common to a music hall than a convention cubicle. The lighting was recessed, letting each painter focus on his or her individual palette.

The seating, too, came in semi-circles, so that Manny could easily keep himself amused by studying the dimmed faces of the others in his circle when the instructor lost his attention, or when he felt that his little palette and board were balanced securely enough on his lap that he could chance to daydream in their direction.

In fact, Manny had been looking in every direction but the instructor's. He didn't even know whether it was a man or woman, someone young or old, quiet or loud, studied or carefree. It seemed that only a silhouette had been speaking up there, using props as if they were pointers to another world. Manny sat watching only the slides: images of unearthly color, so they seemed, for the microscopic cross sections of living cells, minerals, and crystals showed the audience things they had never seen.

Make a thin wash with cadmium yellow. Step through and see what lies behind it. Lay in a dab of alizarin crimson at a corner, and drag it into the yellow. Use the crimson to lay the groundwork for capillaries, the link to your past...

Manny looked up. The instructor looked wide-eyed into the audience. He had seen those intelligent, dark eyes before; they belonged to the woman he had noticed the previous evening, at the keynote address. They looked into him, and all the others in the room disappeared. When she spoke, it was as if she were speaking only to him:

"Take a look inside the colors you have drawn: they are what's inside you. Now. Watch me. Paint like *this*. Let what's inside be your guide. See where it leads you. To forgotten ancestors, perhaps? To part of you that's been lost? Now look here..."

What was she saying, and why were the others sitting there so calmly, as if her words reflected nothing deeper than surface paint? And now she descended from the stage to check on everyone's work. He watched her back and soft shoulders, the gentle way she stooped and the unwavering concentration with which she answered questions. There was something not so like Ellen, but like someone else, someone who attracted him in mysterious ways. As she approached his seat, stopping along the way to talk with others, pointing out something here and there, or using her hands to gesticulate a point, she began to seem more familiar, the only other person in the room.

"Step into the color, the deep color rich with time. Nothing will be faded, or lost."

Manny looked up and saw her standing over him; her brown eyes did not blink, but took him into them, so that he now saw the world in their shades of sepia, sienna, and dark umber.

They went for a noontime walk through the city, which had been darkened by a yellowish fog. She spoke very little, but knew where they should go.

"Where are you from?" Manny said.

"Argentina. But—" She stopped to look around, as if trying to locate something. "My ancestors came from Italy."

"Really?"

"Yes. There are quite a few of us there. Moment—" She turned her head. "Over there."

"In Argentina?"

"No. It is where we will eat."

"How—"

"Shhh." She put her finger to his lips.

Three men in dark clothes and stained caps watched them approach the doorway; beyond them and the entrance there was only fog.

"You'll like this food," she said. "They don't make it like this anymore."

"And why do they make it like this today?" he answered.

"Because you're here."

They ducked through the lines of hanging wooden beads at the entrance and found a room so simply furnished, with only six tables, that Manny wondered whether they had any regular clientele.

"We're here," she said, leading them to a table off-center that she seemed to have reserved. Manny took his seat, but she excused herself immediately to the ladies' room. A waiter appeared from nowhere with a carafe of red wine; he set it on their table without looking at Manny, and disappeared again.

A number of other customers appeared, all of them men, coming in single file from the entrance and fog. The first wore an expression of indescribable sorrow and wit, his eyes focused loosely but steadily before him, left arm holding a mortar trowel. The second came stepping more lively, his face brilliant with a sense of courage and adventure. Another man, much younger than the first two, showed both bewilderment and pride—in his thick arms he carried his sleeping infant son.

Others came, and they walked past Manny to the deepest end of the room, where they were obscured by a dim light.

"Has anyone else come in?" she asked, taking her seat.

"Yes," he said. "A small group of men came in."

"Where?" She looked around. They were gone.

"Perhaps you were daydreaming," she said, with an attractive accent that he had only now begun to notice.

"I wonder."

"But of course, what does it matter?" she concluded. "It's a lovely place for daydreams, isn't it?"

"Any place is good for daydreams. It's one of my favorite pastimes."

"Mine too," she answered. "In fact, I live by them."

Soon a large, ruddy hand appeared before their eyes; it held a fat lamb chop.

"*Signore, signora. Va bene, eh? Sono assai belle.*"

The chef's other hand swung over the table, offering three or four types of freshly-cut *maccherone*. From his pocket he then produced a dark red tomato. Manny smiled; his heart was in his throat at the sight of food so fresh and pure. In fact, the very air of the restaurant had lost its urban dust. Now it smelled of burning pinewood and wild anise, of rosemary and mountain water. It didn't matter that they were the only two dining. What was the rest of the world if not read through the eyes of the moment they were living? An illusion? A memory? Certainly nothing as real, nothing that could touch their senses all at once the way this magical lunch did.

When it was over they walked back through the busy streets of Pittsburgh. The fog had reappeared, obscuring them and providing distance between them where once there had been none, providing another illusion to replace the one they had left.

CHAPTER 12

BUON GIORNO, PIETRO.

Hey you, Pete!

Take it easy; sit down. The world, she's spinning without you. Sometimes you hitch a ride, and she takes you to her other side. Sometimes she spits you back, and you don't know if you are living or daydreaming.

"I'm running. I'm running all over the Earth. Over her waters, too. I'm running in my sleep, trying to find my wife and family. I'm afraid they will be running too, and I won't know to which corner of the world they've run."

Pietro, vieni qua. Here you go. Come home. It's the late summer sun going out now behind Arazecca, and time to count your blessings, time to tally it all up: what you've done with your life.

"I haven't done anything but count seconds, make sure I can survive the next. I gave up on plans; I gave up on looking at the evening sky. The world has had much to tell me, but I haven't had time to listen. It was always a whisper behind the noise. In America, there is always noise."

Don't you remember? *No ti ricordi, tempo fa,* when you were a boy in Castello? You had plans then. You were going to marry Sabina with the blonde hair and generous breasts. Live in Nonno Fiorentino's house after he passed away. Have as many children as it would hold; raise them on healthy abruzzese wine and lamb. Go hunting for boar and rabbit every Saturday afternoon. Play cards in the piazza on Sundays. Let it be known that yours were the finest shoes in town…

"But in America the winters are cold. The leather they use is different. It's not quality that counts, but speed. It's not how you walk, but where you go. Not your ancestors' breath, but your children's, that counts.

"In Castello you worked for the day. You made something with your hands, and someone in the town would buy it, and you'd see your work every day all around town: people wearing your shoes, wearing your days, walking around their days in them. We had something in common then. We were all related by our work."

Work! Work is God is America. Work for work's sake, and none other. Work for money. Work for deception. Work to have as many things as America says you need. Work to avoid loneliness, avoid your neighbor, avoid all responsibility that is not bought. Come, Pietro, to America, to learn everything over, to drain your ancient blood and replace it with ours.

"It's another work, then. A different kind of work. Not for something you can see in people's faces, but for a cold coin in your pocket. Everyone's leveled out by that coin. Maybe it's a good thing, this leveling out, but no one will ever know the price we're paying for that coin."

É caro, Pietro. Very dear. And you're not the first to pay it. You can hear the jingle in their pockets when they return; you can see the jingle in their walk. But with it always comes the furrow in the forehead that never smiles with the eyes. And with it comes children that are anxious, and wives that live by anxiety. Come, Pietro. Send your heart back to Castello, even if your mind and soul must stay somewhere else.

"We had anxiety in Castello, too. A distant anxiety — wondering if we'd be able to get by another year. But for the moment we were always content. And when you live moment by moment time passes slowly, like a gift. It was that gift that kept us from leaving too soon."

America's gifts are generous. They will be passed down to future generations.

"The gift of our ancient home cannot be replaced. It will linger like a ghost in our eyes."

"Your eyes," she said. "There's something familiar about them."

"And yours too."

It was the end of a long convention day. They sat by a wide window that reflected evening sunlight onto their faces, quietly sipping their clear drinks.

"I want you to tell me what's in them," she continued.

"My eyes?" he said.

"Yes. They are full of stories."

"I don't think so. My life hasn't been that interesting."

"Maybe there are stories in them that are yet to come."

Manny smiled. The future. Now that was a book with blank pages, without an end.

"I don't know where to begin."

"Begin with what you're feeling."

"Now?"

"Right now."

"Right now I could tell you the story of a man who doesn't know whether to call himself young or not, who doesn't remember what it means to have a clear mind, and a clear heart with which to love. This man has a couple of children and a nice home to keep them in, with a nice wife that has a deep memory of love attached to her. In fact, nearly everything that this man thinks and feels these days is attached to a memory. These memories are growing heavy in him. And he's not sure where they are calling from, what they mean."

"I know what they mean," she said. His eyes were still. "They mean that you are not looking to the future, or even the present."

"Yes," he replied, "but I think I'm getting better, because I'm enjoying the present with you."

"Then tell me more about you. What about your work, your passions?"

Manny went blank, not knowing whether his thoughts were his own. He felt some stock explanations rising in his mind, but also felt deeper things stirring inside, things he had never before attempted to find. It was as if this woman were handing him a moment that was without constraints, without anxiety.

"My work brought me here, or at least that's what I'm supposed to believe. But the truth is, my history brought me here, and my willingness to face it down. I need to learn more about that history. I have to say I feel lost in this city, as if I'd never grown up here. I need to rediscover it."

He continued:

"I live in Berkeley, you know, and work in San Francisco. There are times that I feel connected to my work, deeply, so that I lose myself in what I'm doing, and feel pride at the end of the day. Other times I wonder why I'm living there, or why I'm living at all. I wonder why I don't drive home at ten thirty and meet my wife to make love, or pick up my kids from school and take them to feed the seals."

"And why don't you?" Her great eyes were still as she spoke. "Why don't you do what you want to do?"

He straightened, then fell relaxed again:

"I-I don't know. I feel a tension on those days. I don't know what's expected of me, or what I expect of myself. Most days I don't care about expectations—I never did. And now, at times, I do. Is this what happens when you feel your youth is over? Then time isn't what it used to be. It's no longer endless. Then your past melds with your parents', and their parents' past, and so on, until you reach back and find a certain emptiness that you long to fill…"

He stopped short, and felt that emptiness even now beginning to overtake him again.

"I feel that I'm talking too much," he said. "What about you? Tell me about yourself."

"Oh," she began calmly, and with utter sincerity, "I never talk about myself."

"Why not?"

"I'd lose myself, and anyone I was talking to."

Manny creased his brow and looked past her. For a moment she disappeared.

"Is there something wrong?" she asked.

The sun had finally set, and her face looked ordinary without its last rays falling over it. She drew from a cigarette that had been lighted all along, though Manny hadn't noticed it.

"No. Nothing's wrong," he said.

"I'm afraid I'm very tired. See you tomorrow then?"

"Yes. Good night."

"*Buona notte.*"

The next thing he noticed was the lights being turned on. The bar was closing, and he hadn't realized how long he'd been sitting there, alone.

CHAPTER 13

"HERE I AM!"

That is all they heard, from every corner of the bar, when he entered. It was a loud pronouncement, in English, by a foreign tongue, and for that reason they welcomed him as one of their own.

Italians were few in the bar, however. They were Germans, for the most part; some Czechs, a few Slovaks, and a fair number of Poles. Pietro, smiling, saw his friend Karl raise an arm to wave him over to the bar, where a draft already awaited him.

"You come, Pietro. Good, good!"

"Eh, too many shoe make me a headache."

"Here you go. Now this will get rid of that headache."

"And then give you another," said the man seated next to Karl.

They laughed.

"Some time, the wine too," Pietro said.

"This is my friend Pietro. *Ein guter Mensch.* He never stays out late. A good family man. But I see that light in his eyes. He's not all perfect, you see."

More laughter came over them. Pietro took a seat at the bar, feeling the pressure pull back from his tired feet as he raised them off the floor. Within the half-hour he felt he had been lifted off the ground completely — it was a feeling he welcomed, because it took time and its menacing oppression away from him. He felt he could have been living there all his life, and that the rest had been nothing but recurring dreams.

These Germans liked to laugh, though their laughter was not like Italian laughter, with its shrill abandonment of contained emotion. Rather, German laughter was explosive, and nearly predictable in its duration. But the most impressive thing for Pietro was that there was so much laughter at all, no matter what wretched race was producing it.

As the evening went on, and Karl went on ordering rounds for everyone, it became evident that something was missing: women. Pietro had closed his eyes and let them stay shut for as long as it took to soothe them from another long day.

"Hey Pete, meet Magda."

His dizziness ended abruptly. A new scent warmed the air, and the eyes of a woman looked at him from across the corner of the bar.

Until now, non-Italians had held a limited space in Pietro's mind, one that was not taken very seriously; for they could never be as honorable, as loyal, as creative or enduring as his race. Who, after all, had given more to the world than the Italians?

"Magda is from Heidelberg. But her English isn't so bad."

"You are here before the war?" Pietro asked.

"Oh, yes, yes — long before that. I came with my parents in the twenties —"

She was interrupted by one of Karl's loud German friends, and Pietro's original view of Germans returned for a moment, before vanishing again as he watched the lovely blonde tilt her head when she spoke.

"Pete! What are you looking at?"

"*Scusa?*"

Pietro hailed the bartender:

"A drink for the lady, *prego!*"

"Ah, now that's the way," Karl bellowed. His thick German hand landed on Pietro's back, and Pietro merely shrugged it off, while laughing.

"Ah!" Pietro called. "But she must drink it with me." He smiled widely. "And then we will dance." Or maybe, thought Pietro, they will dance now, drink later. He pushed his way past a couple of tall Slovaks to the young lady, whose back had been turned to him. He slipped his arm through hers and pulled her away.

"Come. We will ask the man to play an Italian song."

Before Magda could catch her breath Pietro had convinced the piano man to launch into a stately *tarantella* (the only song Pietro knew), even humming a few lines to make sure it was the right one.

"Do what I do," he commanded, and the German girl responded with a little smile that endeared her to him all the more. Pietro spun her hand, and she nearly lost her balance, but tried to follow along for at least the first couple of minutes.

"Okay, I am tired," she said. Hearing no response from him she repeated the plea, but by now Pietro had been transported back to his youth, and both his hearing and sight had become very selective. He took her hand and pushed it up into the air, holding her waist close to his. She felt she was becoming sick, so undid his arm and pulled herself away, falling back toward the piano, and catching herself on its rim. The music stopped and Magda made her way back to friends at the bar, but Pietro kept dancing.

"Eh! Come back! It's not finished! Come, come!"

"Get lost," she muttered.

Pietro threw his hands up and raced back to her, a new fire lighting up his eyes. But they were soon extinguished by a man's fist, and he fell back onto the floor.

"Babbo, babbo. Sentimi. Babbo!"

Pina stood over the slumped-over Pietro as he struggled to stay awake under the hot light of the kitchen.

"Come on, Babbo. We'll get you to bed before Mamma wakes up."

Pietro winked at her and smiled.

"Don't worry, Pina," he mumbled. "Almerinda will not know about it. Just lead me to bed — a good girl you are, *Pinuccia. Brava.*"

She helped him one step at a time to the dark landing between stairs. There they rested before looking up and seeing Almerinda standing at the top of the second set, arms folded over her heavy nightgown. Her silver hair fell braided down her back, and her mouth was very tightly shut.

"Go to bed, Pina. I'll take him." It was a commanding voice she rarely used, so Pina obliged. She walked hesitantly back to her room and closed her door after entering, catching a glimpse of her mother's contracted face and her father's stone smile. Then, straining to hear from her bed, she caught Almerinda's voice beginning in its low resonant tones, and rising steadily to louder bursts, with only a mumble or two every now and then coming from her poor father.

"Giuseppina," Jim whispered beside her. "What's going on?"

"Nothing. Go to sleep."

Pina rose at dawn the next day, as she normally did, and passed Almerinda — who had sat in the chair in the hallway all night — without saying a word. She decided to cook breakfast for everyone that day, but when she called them no one came except Jim.

Chapter 14

On the last afternoon of the conference Manny skipped off to Shadyside, a cultural outpost of town, to buy gifts for his family. While surveying some jewelry displayed by an outdoor vendor he heard his name ring, twice, before looking around.

"Manny. Hey — Manny!"

It was his cousin Ray, who had grown up in the same neighborhood as Manny, who was a couple of years older, who always knew everything, and who never failed to have opinions that were hewn from stone. But something about Ray's self-assurance had always attracted Manny, who only pretended to see things as clearly.

"Come on," Ray ordered after their genuine embrace, "I'll buy you lunch."

"Cigar?"

"No, thanks." Manny said too quickly, then reconsidered: "Well, maybe." It was as if he felt that not accepting it would mean not being part of the family, though he was beginning to wonder what part of the family Ray represented.

There were hints of Manny's uncles in Ray, and even a distant shadow of their grandfather, but the sparkle in Ray's eyes had gone out. He was now living the perfect dream of their ancestors: a lawyer with a comfortable practice, a family in a respectable suburb, a correct haircut and suit, but Manny found nothing interesting in him.

In the presence of Ray, Manny didn't know whether to feel ashamed or relieved about his own life. On a scorecard he would have fared at least as well: the marriage, house, kids, etc., but his life was still less certain. He couldn't see it all at once, only in bits, in individual actions and relationships. How could Ray sit there so smugly? Wasn't there anything that could bring a little panic to his eyes?

"How do you like these shoes?" Manny said, holding his right leg up beside the table.

"What?"

"Aren't they great? Only seventy-five bucks. Not bad for this kind of quality."

Ray looked at Manny's foot dangling in the air, booted with a dull black, heavy-soled casual.

"Yeah, they're fine. Are we having dessert? How about cappuccino? They make a great cup here."

"It's funny about shoes," Manny went on. "I feel completely different wearing every pair I've ever owned. When you think about it, they're the only thing that keeps us from touching the earth completely, from being rooted there."

"So?"

"So they're what makes us human, different, cut off from other living things that touch this planet naked their whole lives."

"What about horses?"

"Horses?"

"Yeah. They wear shoes."

Manny delighted in this newly discovered sense of humor, but Ray's face remained thoughtful. He was serious.

"That's...not the same," Manny stumbled. Then, after a long pause: "I think I will have dessert."

They bade goodbye outside the restaurant, on a sidewalk that was congested with others hurrying back to work. Ray had wanted to show Manny "the office," but Manny too had to get back to his appointed place and time. And even though his hotel room had nothing of the history that Ray's handshake held, he preferred to go back there and dwell in the unending present.

During his ride back to town Manny sank deeply into his bones; his eyelids closed lightly, and his folded hands dropped out of his lap. The bus's hum went off and on, off and on. Passing trees blocked the sunlight intermittently, so that Manny's closed eyelids went from black to orange to black.

His childhood bus rides came back to him: excursions to a baseball game at Forbes Field, or a shopping trip he took with his mother downtown. Bus rides were uncontrollable things that brought you to a controllable destination; all along the ride you were offered free views of other corners of the city, places you could never imagine because they were so different from the place that was yours.

This life of Manny's was one uncontrollable destination, a ride through vistas of his past as translated by the present. Staring up at him from a crowded streetcorner was Ray, in his attorney's uniform and demeanor, but with a dim recollection laying low in the eyes: the eyes of Pietro, their great-grandfather, who had brought them all here. Those eyes drifted by, but reappeared in the window next to Manny, a reflection of his own eyes, where Pietro resided as well.

And then Manny thought: "Am I to be him, then? Am I just his projection, aimless, uncertain, but guided by a past conscience?"

Heavier trees passed by, and large, dark buildings. The route had changed. The road grew bumpy, and soon the blank hum of tires rolling over bricks could be heard. Manny looked around and realized that he was the only passenger on the bus. He wondered if he had taken the wrong one—where was it taking him? And then the bus slowed, pulling off to the side of the road.

"This is the end of the line, buddy."

"Oh. Where am I?" Manny asked.

The driver waved as he descended the steps, and then disappeared into a line of wooden row homes. Manny walked up the empty aisle to the door and came down the three steep steps to a part of Pittsburgh he had never seen before.

The row homes looked strong and well-kept, though most were unpainted, and all had been blown with a fine, black dust. When Manny looked up he saw the dust blowing above them in slow swirls. The dust faded the sunlight, and the only warmth seemed to come from inside the homes. A sash flew up on the second story of the house he stood before, and a woman's hand, pale at the end of a black sleeve, reached up to close it. Before Manny's eyes had left the window the front door opened, and the stately middle-aged woman in black beckoned him in.

She led him through a stark hallway to the kitchen, then put her finger to her lips to tell him he should observe the quiet. In a bedroom adjacent to the kitchen lay a snoring man, spread-eagled on the bed, deep in his siesta. He wore no pants; nothing but a large, stained shirt covered him. It occurred to Manny that they might have made love that afternoon, before his arrival.

No less than six children, from about three to ten years old, came into the room from a back door, teasing and torturing one another with verbal abuses. They spoke in English, but some of the abuses were in Italian. Some danced around the table as others deftly maneuvered through some boxes in a cupboard for cookies.

"Shoo, shoo!" said the mother, who had been cleaning her pasta maker with a brush.

"So now," began another voice from a man who sat across the table, who seemed no older than Manny, "what did you expect to find here?"

"Me?" Manny said. "Nothing."

"Eh!" he laughed. "He says nothing!" He spoke with a thick Italian accent. His hair, dark and shiny, was uncombed. There were stars in his eyes, which were circled by darkness and topped by a finely chiseled brow. "Then I will ask you," he continued, "why you have walked here, and what kind of shoes you wore?"

Manny looked down and found, to his surprise, that his feet were bare, smooth as the day he'd been born.

"I—funny—I didn't realize I wasn't wearing any!"

"Why you don't wear shoes? Everybody need them, even an old man with nothing left to do. I will make you a pair—and you will wear them until you die."

"But you don't even know me," Manny resisted.

"No important. Soon you will see."

The man brought up a box from under the table and began unloading various Old World tools—tools for cutting and shaping leather, for sewing it together and punching holes in it, for polishing and lacing it. Manny watched in astonishment, for the man's hand worked so quickly that time seemed to be passing at double speed. Once or twice he caught the sound of the children haggling in another room, or of the wife scurrying about, but he could never take his eyes away from the shoes that were evolving before him. They were just about done.

Then something quite unexpected happened. The shoemaker took the new shoes, and put them on his own feet.

Manny was puzzled: "I thought they were supposed to be mine."

"Yes, they are. But I have to make sure they fit."

"But how—"

"My shoes are your shoes."

Now Manny noticed that the shoes this man had been wearing were identical to the new ones he had just slipped on. Perhaps he had made them also.

"Here," the shoemaker said. "Now wear my shoes." He took off the newer shoes and handed them to Manny, who put them on and noted, with satisfaction, that they were a perfect fit.

"You will know why you have come now. Very soon, you will know."

CHAPTER 15

IN THE SKY MANNY FELT REMOVED FROM MORE than the earth. He felt removed from himself, and his past, from everything he had known. He felt as if he were between worlds again, the way he felt when he and Ellen had first moved West.

With their move West had come a move in the way they viewed things. For Manny, it was a final release of all he had been taught about societal norms. He had to rethink everything, swim daily through uncharted waters, and he rather liked it. It made him feel necessary, singled him out among the endless generations of sleepwalkers who never thought or did anything other than what their ancestors had done. The kind of household he and Ellen found themselves running could not have been anything like the households their parents and grandparents had run.

And it's funny, Pietro had thought exactly the same thing while lying awake the first night in his American bed. This adventure, he decided, would vindicate his manhood, allow him to take a special seat among the stars for his bravery. He saw now a long line of his progeny, boys taller and stronger than they had ever been in Castello, and girls with beautiful complexions and determined eyes. Who knows what kingdoms they would build? Would they own automobiles, and drive around this land as if it belonged to them? Everything in America was green, everything growing uncontrollably, without regard to what or who came yesterday. Pietro would break himself to become a part of it. He would not be afraid, and his fearless nature would be transferred first to Almerinda, then to his children, and their children. This was a night of awakening, a night of awakening to dreams that would not leave him with the new light.

"Ellen?"

No response.

"Ellen!" he shouted again, "I'm home!"

But she didn't answer. There were signs of Ellen (shoes in the foyer, newspaper spread on the dining room table, emptied grocery bag on the kitchen counter) but there was no Ellen. Had he told her when he'd be home? Did his mind slip, as it sometimes did, and make him say Tuesday instead of Monday? But that was not the worst part. The worst part was that he was beginning to like coming home to this quiet snapshot of his former life. He had only just begun thinking of that life as "former," though he knew that nothing had changed to make it anything else. Unless of course Jo had grown up in the course of these few days, and Sam had lost a molar or two. And the driveway had finally caved in.

Chances are none of these things had happened. He began looking for something to do, to appear occupied when Ellen finally did come home and find him there so relaxed, and innocent. He even rehearsed the impending conversation:

"Oh, didn't I say I'd be home today?"

"You certainly *did not*. Do you think I wouldn't remember that? And what was so on your mind there, anyway, that you couldn't even keep the date straight?"

"Nothing. What do you mean..."

And so forth. He imagined it wouldn't degenerate into an argument, but a playful release of the tension that builds when two people are separated. They'd probably end up making love that night, though not in more than the usual way. He imagined this scene while drifting off on that new, wide couch in the family room, because he really could think of nothing better to do than take a nap.

He awoke to her voice. She was bending down to him.

"Manny? Wake up."

And then:

"Hi Daddy," with a womanish kiss on the cheek.

"Hey Dad, what'd you get me?" Sam sat on his legs.

"Did you say you'd be home today?" Ellen asked, genuinely puzzled.

"I sure did."

"Oh," she said in one little breath, "I guess I'm losing it. We've been having meetings every afternoon this week, and I'm *exhausted*."

"What about?"

"Oh, Ron's got this idea that we're not concentrating on the right kinds of research—I mean we're not after the big breakthrough kind of stuff, like drug-resistant bacteria. I have to say I agree with him this time. We're really seeing eye-to-eye on a lot of things—"

"Mummy, cut the crap. What's for dinner?" Jo stood with her arms folded and eyes unwavering.

Ellen looked at Manny and threw her hands up: "Ask your father."

"Don't look at me. I'm jet-lagged, remember?"

"Oh, I guess you are. Let's see. We have hot dogs, Firebrick pizza, eggs..."

"Let's have scrambled eggs," said Sam.

"I'm going to McDonald's," Manny said. "Anyone coming?"

"I'll probably be in bed when you get home," Ellen reported as she walked to the stairwell. "I'm really tired. I don't know if I can stay up."

Manny took the cue.

He and Sam sat near a bright window eating their Quarter Pounders as Jo made herself eggs at home and Ellen scrutinized the little lines around her eyes before turning down the bed. She was not hungry.

71

Thus ended Manny's return home. Not that he was expecting much, but the disappointment of not having a good meal or anyone to ask him about his trip seemed to weigh more heavily this time, as if there were another Manny living in another dimension who had been granted these things as a matter of course, while our Manny had been denied them.

"Are you going to eat your fries, Dad?"

Manny half-heard Sam, who at seven was already showing signs of following in his footsteps for having a hearty appetite.

"Go ahead. We'll split them."

Even McDonald's was beginning to look different to him, like a frame in a color comic strip. The bodies moving through it were prerecorded cutouts from some marketing mastermind, and Manny felt like the only reader. Even Sam, so intently chewing his fries and sucking up his milkshake, fit seamlessly into the scene. Manny had to pull his son out of it.

"Hurry up. We have to go shopping."

"I think Mom went yesterday."

"Not food, Sam. Fishing rods."

Manny watched his son's mouth open and close, its reckless assault on the culinary contents. He was beginning to wonder about the response (they had never gone fishing before) but finally Sam shrugged, reached for the shake, and said, "okay."

"First," Manny began, "we need to buy wading boots."

The bed that night was safe and warm, but Manny wanted daring and tempestuous. He curled around the sleeping Ellen and began licking her back. His hand wandered over her silken body, finding the plush spot on the other side of her thigh and the softer skin buried there.

"What are you doing?" she mumbled.

He hushed her, and continued his manipulations. Her protests became less frequent, and he was finally able to persuade her to complete the event. The covers thrown back, they made love in the usual way, though Manny's movements were more creative than she remembered from previous episodes. When it was over they both went for a glass of water and returned to bed. Ellen pulled the covers up to her neck and assumed the curled position he had found her in earlier. Manny lay on his back with his hands behind his head, humming a tune he'd heard on the radio on the way back from McDonald's.

"Ellen?"

She grunted.

"I was a little disappointed that there was no dinner for me tonight. I mean, after my trip and all."

First there was an infinite pause, then she reawakened with a garrulous laugh.

"Well?" he continued.

She did finally turn to him: "Well, what?"

"Well why didn't you?"

"Why? Because, I don't know, because I had to pick up the kids late, do some shopping, make some phone calls—I didn't get home until after you did. You're a better cook anyway."

"That's not the point."

"What's the point?"

"The point is I was tired and away from home for a few days, and it would have been nice. That's all."

"Okay. Well I'm sorry. Next time."

"Ah, don't worry about it."

"I am worried about it. Now you have me all upset."

He noted that familiar shift in her tone that meant he was losing ground. The old Manny would have reassured her of the unimportance of the transgression, thereby resolving her from any moral ambiguity. But the new Manny remained silent, and they both drifted into a sleepless sleep, regarding the column of chilly air that separated them down the middle of the bed.

CHAPTER 16

As PART OF A GENERAL RESTRUCTURING OF THE EASTBOUND streetcar service, the Port Authority had decided to redirect, extend, or discontinue certain lines. The streetcar Pietro usually took home from work, for instance, now took a sharp turn to go through a neighborhood Pietro had never seen before. Pietro cursed and rang the bell, demanding an explanation. The conductor slowed and pointed to the notice which he said had been hanging in front of everybody's nose for weeks now, and why hadn't Pietro read it? To this Pietro's line of expletives increased in Italo-English to the point that the conductor had to ask him to get off. Pietro threw his cap at the sparking monster as it rattled away from him in its unfamiliar direction.

Damn it, damn them, damn everything, Pietro thought. He would walk home, whether he knew the way or not. It was another infernal August night in Pittsburgh, and maybe it wouldn't be a bad idea to walk by the river — it led him in the right direction, after all.

Now the sun still sat high enough in the yellowish sky to allow him time to pause. He watched the dark, dead water roll past, wondering if any fish had ever lived in it, wondering whether the young Germans, Irish, and Scots of Pittsburgh had ever spent a day of doing nothing but turning over rocks and fishing. Then Pietro split in two: one of him stole back to the main avenue and briskly headed home, but the other put his hand in the water and stooped to see his reflection. One did not need to know how to read and write to struggle with nature. One did not need an angry, wobbly machine to get you from one place to another. And one did not need electric lights when there was the sun. Pietro saw a changing face in the water, one with a long, frothy beard and aimless hair. It was the face of Fiorentino, who had been dead longer than Pietro had been married. Even after the face had disappeared, Pietro heard his grandfather warning him again:

"Now you watch, pretty soon they'll be bringing newspapers to Castello and making everyone glum with their bad news."

Pietro looked deeply into the water, and returned:

"You're right, Nonno. The newspaper is everywhere. You have to read just to get by. A man can't rely on his own wits in this damned country."

"Beware of the city, Pietro, where God is lost and people think they have a right to do as they please. Everyone is suspicious, because they live without faith in one another."

"Great words for a small boy," Pietro mumbled. For it was true: books and newspapers must be read because people didn't have the time to speak to one another. All the men in dark suits running around downtown were like dry wells, empty of good stories, with nothing to pass on to their grandsons. Even Pietro felt himself too tired to speak when he came home. The well in him was also running dry, and anger was filling in the place where words once grew.

He rose and let the river continue. Fiorentino sank back down to its unknowable depth, and this Pietro reunited with his other self, turning back to the streets of commerce and packed homes, a place where he and his family, like the others, drank in the newness of America daily, without having time to reflect on what it was.

The long walk had done Pietro good. He was no longer angry at the streetcar and its driver, and no longer melancholy for the loss of Fiorentino's times. He felt now the way he'd felt in his younger days at Castel di Sangro, after a long walk home from their mountain cabin to the valley.

Almerinda said nothing of the late hour, but immediately shot off a command that they should go to her friend Assunta's house to see the new *macchina* they'd bought.

"What kind of *macchina?*" Pietro asked.

"*La macchina, la macchina,*" Almerinda repeated. "The one you drive, you know."

Pietro had seen (and cursed) them, yes, taking over the ways people used to walk on, making noise and blowing ever more black smoke into the filthy American sky.

"You go. I don't care 'bout."

"Put your hat on. I said we were coming."

"I don't feel well."

Almerinda returned with silence and total disregard, a cue Pietro understood well enough to mean he would lose this argument, and possibly connubial privileges for a length of time, if he didn't come along.

Assunta, unable to contain herself, came ducking like a chicken down the walkway that led from her front door to the sidewalk. Her brownish hair, powdered white under certain slants of light, seemed to glow with the force of her excitement.

"*Venite! Venite!*" she called, even as Almerinda ran up to take her hand. She too was growing more animated, and Pietro couldn't imagine why all the fuss.

"Pietro, come around back," was the latest command he heard, this time from Massimo, who had met them coming down the driveway.

"*O Dio Madonna!*" Almerinda exhaled. "Pietro—look, look."

Pietro saw it, yes, and though it looked in perfect condition he saw nothing more remarkable about it. Massimo caressed its hood and fenders as Assunta looked on like a new mother. After a reverent moment of silence Massimo produced the key, and insisted they go for a ride.

"Not long," Almerinda said. Pietro nodded, and reluctantly went in.

The seat was surprisingly comfortable, he thought, and as they backed out of the driveway he began to see how perfectly the pieces of this automobile fit together. It reminded him of his shoes, and he wondered who was responsible for this new kind of craftsmanship.

Massimo eagerly led them away from the busiest streets to a boulevard that ran beside the river. They felt a cooler air rush in through the car's open windows, and were quite content to finish off the hot day this way. Little was said, though Massimo hummed to himself and nodded politely to several other drivers in their sleek black sedans. He felt he had finally arrived at a certain degree of success by driving his car, and Pietro too was beginning to feel pride in being part of the scene.

"Toot the horn, Massimo," his wife insisted.

"Horn? Why?"

"*Dai! Dai!*" she returned.

Massimo felt around for the button and pressed it two or three times. Assunta raised her brow and smiled. Massimo turned around to look at Pietro and Almerinda in the back seat, this time holding down the button for a few seconds. Almerinda began laughing uncontrollably, and Assunta shouted above the horn:

"See, how nice she sounds?"

Another driver came up around the left side to pass them and Massimo tooted even louder. Pietro threw in a couple of loud words and had everyone laughing again.

"Hey you, piss off!" Massimo repeated, having liked hearing Pietro say it so well. Then Assunta joined him, as well as Pietro again. Almerinda could barely catch her breath.

"You see," Massimo managed to calm down enough to say. "Every ride is a great adventure. God bless America, eh, Pietro?"

"Right. And God bless me, the shoemaker. *L'americano.*"

Pietro went home to dream of a quiet river that became wider and wider as he tried to swim across it. Mountains rose and fell on its distant side, and voices murmured to him from under the soft waves. "When I die," he said to his wife the next morning, "don't spend money on my funeral." She looked at him quizzically. "Just tie me in a sack and throw me in the river."

CHAPTER 17

"*FISHING?*"

Ellen stood with her arms folded, assuming that phony June Cleaver stance that meant she meant to play the role.

"Yeah, fishing," Manny loudly returned.

"But you've never even been fishing before. How do you know—"

"And how do you know what I've done and haven't done before? I had a life before we got together, just like you. We used to skip school and go fishing. Half the teachers went too."

"Must be a boy thing."

"Maybe it is a boy thing. And since Sam and I are both boys we're going fishing tomorrow."

"It's a school day."

"We're going just the same."

That particular little grilling irritated Manny more than usual—he didn't know why. It had more to do with something inside him, his view of himself, though, than it had to do with her. He kissed her cheek, neck, and back several times before leaving the bed so early the following morning. (He couldn't imagine waking without the opportunity to do so.) She didn't awaken, but a smile passed over her lips.

The drive to Mount Shasta was long, but it gave Manny the opportunity to become lost in the moving view, as Sam snored in the back seat. He drove without music, without a schedule to keep, without even having eaten a good breakfast. He purposely took back roads, so he might see what he'd never seen before. A late-summer rain had come during the past week, and spots of green could already be seen on certain hillsides as they moved out of the valley.

Manny had forgotten how clear the roads could be on a Wednesday morning. Did no one else have business to attend to? Where were the loggers, the vintners, the commuting schoolteachers? The only company seemed to be sheep, and an occasional darting bird. What was he left to do but remember his dream?

The first remembered image threw a pang into his heart: there she was, solidly sexy, lying half out of the covers, a smile of contentment on her lips. They had made love, there in his own house, in his own bed, freely and happily. But now he remembers why the aftermath was not entirely pleasant—this woman was not his wife. How could he have dreamt of her, when he couldn't even remember her name? But the eyes were unmistakably hers, the skin, the quiet fall of dark hair. Was it Regina, Flora, Maria? All names seemed equal to him as he tried to remember; all names pointless, in vain. For it wasn't only her he couldn't name, but his desire for her, a desire half-hidden in an early morning dream. What else lay hidden inside him, waiting for a carefree moment so it could surface?

He was only now beginning to realize that the woman he'd met in Pittsburgh was the sum of these moments, moments he'd had upon awakening, at insufferable board meetings, even while eating a solitary lunch. They were only an extension of him, something that should not be brushed aside, or bring shame.

Others must have these moments too. Sexual longing must represent only a part of them, a piece of a greater whole. The whole was something that was missing in your life, something you couldn't name, and so it came up in memorable images at the most unpredictable times. And was there a way to find the missing something, and make it part of your conscious, everyday life? At least, thought Manny, he'd been granted the gift of knowing it existed.

Sammy stirred in the back seat, and Manny grew tense with the realization that he was a father, a firm role which left little room for things that could not be named.

"Are we there?"

"No. Almost. Close your eyes."

"I'm not tired anymore."

"Then count something."

"What should I count?"

"I don't know. Trees."

"There aren't any."

"There will be. Look ahead."

A distant slope showed furry green as it rose to the speckled snowcap of Mount Shasta. Sammy lost himself in his seven-year-old thoughts, while Manny tried his best to keep work projects from intruding on his. Within a half-hour they had arrived at the small lake, tucked into those hills, that Rick had told Manny about at the office. A quiet path led them to a little stream that fed the lake.

"What are we going to catch today?"

Manny looked around quickly, and before he could think further, said, "I don't know."

"Then why did we come?"

"Why? I don't—look—I don't know why. To see things."

"Dad! Come here! Look at this." But by the time Manny made his way over the trout had disappeared, so he went back to the car to find the right tackle for fly fishing. But a loud splashing startled him; he looked back and saw Sammy dancing around in the sparkling water, trying to catch a fish with his hands.

"Sam! Hey!"

"Quiet, Dad. I almost got him."

Manny stole up to the stream again, holding the rods and hips boots he'd gotten from the car. The water ran low and clear over clean, round rocks. Sammy was barefoot in the stream, pants rolled up to his knees.

"Oh my God!" he shouted. "Dad, look at all these little guys. There's millions of them. Come on and look, quick!"

"They're tadpoles."

"Cool. And look at this." He held up the crayfish he'd been carrying by the tail.

"It's a crayfish. I used to find them too. You've seen them before, right?"

"No."

"You mean there aren't any crayfish in Berkeley?"

"Yeah, Dad. And grizzly bears too." A smile passed behind Sammy's eyes and infected Manny, who, until now, had not quite given himself up to a day of freedom. "Okay now. Here's your rod. Have fun."

"Are you going to wear those elephant boots?"

"They're hips boots. You're supposed to—what the hell—how's the water? I'll wade too."

"Yeah Dad. It's fun. And the mud feels all cool and soft."

The morning passed as they stood quietly in the soft mud. Manny gave Sammy a lesson or two, and Sammy caught the first fish: a six-inch perch that slid out of his hands as soon as it was unhooked.

Everywhere, the late-summer life was elusive: trees rustled behind their backs, fish plopped and shivered by, and mosquitoes buzzed invisibly, while dragonflies changed aerial position as quickly as alien spacecraft. Slowly, Manny and his son were enfolded in a secret: a life beyond theirs, one that seemed to come from both inside and outside them.

"I feel like I've been here before," Sammy suddenly said. "What's that called, Dad?"

"*Déja vu.*"

"That's what I'm having. Didja view."

Manny was feeling it too, and was surprised that they were feeling it together.

"How come we never came before?" Sam asked.

"Too busy."

"Let's come again, okay? Hey! Look —"

They had thought they held this world to themselves, but another figure came splashing down the stream, barefoot, leaning over now and then along the way to peer into the water. It was a boy of about ten.

"Hey," Sam said.

"Hey," said the boy. "Anything in particular you're looking for?"

His skin looked to be always under shadow, though his blue-gray eyes sparkled with light. "Because I know where the biggest fish are."

"Are you from around here?" Manny said.

"You might say that. You might say that I know this place better than anyplace else. Up here it don't matter where you're from. You just have to know where the fish are."

"Okay," Manny answered, "so where are they?"

The boy turned and waved them over to the bank, where his muddy sneakers had been lying together under the shade of poplars. Manny and Sam followed him, and put on their own shoes, which felt as if they'd never been worn.

"Dad!" Sammy whispered to his father, "look at his shoes."

But Manny had already noted them, for the boy's shoes were not sneakers at all, but satiny new boots that tied up to his ankles. And for all their size and weight they made little sound trampling along the bank.

The boy's hair had soft golden highlights on its chestnut color, and his gait was easy and free. Manny felt akin to him, and Sam lost all wariness or inhibition near him.

"Much farther?" Manny said. It seemed they had been walking through eternity. But almost as if reading his mind, the boy turned and said: "Here."

Now this stream had opened up, or so it seemed, because sun filled it completely, and few trees stood along its shores. Even the small mounds of grass and stone that broke the water's surface sparkled, giving the scene life beneath its sterile beauty. In another moment, the boy had thrown off his boots and crashed into the water, leaving droplets flying like sparks about him.

"Come on," he said. "The fish are here."

"Let's see who can get the biggest one," Sammy said, entering the water and casting his rod. For a moment Manny stood watching the two boys, their intent faces and agile bodies surrendered to chance. What would strike next? And how would they master the challenge?

"Come on, Dad!"

"In a minute. I'm taking a break."

"We don't have a minute. You gotta see these fish! Man, they're everywhere."

"I know, Sammy. I know. I've seen fish before."

"Not these fish."

Walking into the water again was like moving through a flickering screen for Manny: fish jumped and stones gleamed, and the sun was so bright that Manny could not keep his gaze very long on anything. The result was a steady, slowed reel of sparking frames and the intermittent voices of the boys. To rest his eyes, then, Manny looked down, and felt a strong tug on his line. He looked out again in the direction of his lure and felt the line pulling left and right.

"You got it!" the boy called.

Manny nodded and kept up his concentration, reeling and pulling back, then reeling again. "What—what did I get?"

"The biggest one, the one we've been looking for."

"Oh—" Manny cut himself short when he felt the line go slack. He looked out over the choppy water; a crash like a tree branch falling into the water drew his attention away, where he caught only the wide tail of the jumping monster fish re-entering the stream. He had nothing to say to the boys, feeling that this somehow betrayed his role as the older, instructing sportsman. But the boy spoke up again:

"He does that every time. That's why no one's caught him yet."

"He must be full of holes then," Manny answered, and the boys laughed.

Manny couldn't help seeing that fish again, underwater, probably nipping at his heels and watching him from behind rocks. There was something to be envied about it—was it its erratic life, its beauty and size, or simply its fierce determination? So a fish full of holes stays a fish, he thought, the way a man full of scars less visible stays a man. Was there beauty in that? Beauty in the struggle, the unpredictability of things to come? Now he felt that Ellen should be there with him, that her life too had become predictable and ordered. He wanted her to flash about him, to appear and disappear in random flashes that reflected her life-giving moods. And they could be there together at any time during the day, at night, during any season. The multiplicity of worldly events was reflected in the natural world around him, but he knew that those events were not always chosen, that they must not always be chosen, because that is a certain kind of death. The only way to order the natural world, to which both he and Ellen and everyone else belonged, was to kill it, and start over. Why must there be this relentless starting-over? Wasn't it enough to let it consume them, as it undoubtedly someday would? Manny stood thinking, given up to the water and the sun, and the air that moved between them...

"Dad! I caught 'im. I know I did. Come here!"

Manny waded through the water towards Sammy, who had by now reeled in half his line. The big trout pulled helplessly away, but Manny brought him up with the net. They had caught the Elusive One together, in one split second.

"Let's tell him, Dad. Come on."

Sammy looked everywhere at once, holding his short breath, but the boy was gone. They called for him, but he didn't come. His shoes were gone, his tackle, even his long-sleeved shirt that had been rolled into a ball on the shore. It was as if he'd never come.

"Funny."

"What, Dad?"

"How fast things can happen here."

CHAPTER 18

WHAT IS THERE ABOUT THIS PLACE, Pietro thinks, *that makes us want to stay?* Is there anything left for him to see, or has he already taken it all in, leaving an emptiness in the place inside him that used to be filled with yearning, and wonder? It takes an early morning between dreams for an old man to feel this, for him to measure up who he is and where he's arrived in his long life. In this glimmering consciousness he can almost remember his own distant self-measuring up again—when he was only fourteen. And was there more or less to think about now? So much more has become obvious; the need for worry has disappeared. But the memory of worry—that is what he must connect to this early morning reckoning. He must now conclude whether the worry was worth it, and whether coming to America has sprouted more or less of it.

What is there at the end of a man's life? A feeling akin to floating in space, of looking down and seeing The Whole Story, and not feeling more attached to any one episode over another. That is what Pietro felt one late-summer day in Pittsburgh, half-awake beside his snoring Almerinda. He saw the faces of his children in the dawn-filled windows, and recognized that they belonged neither to Castel di Sangro nor to Pittsburgh; they belonged to Pietro and Almerinda, and to the spirits of all their ancestors. Pina's laugh echoed from their redbrick home all the way across the ocean to Mount Arazecca, and back again. Laughter was something, like tears and tempers, that rolled around in a person to define that person's life. What did it matter whether you faced bald Arazecca or a green Pittsburgh hillside when you awoke?

He'd heard of some success stories from a distant Castello, but he wondered who considered them successful. On which side of the Atlantic were those things to be defined? Was Pietro's success a story that was told back in Castello? Or had people there forgotten him in their own daily struggles and accomplishments? He thought of his boyhood friend, the gypsy Mirko, who wanted to train horses for the circus someday. That was his only wish, his only measure of success. Pietro should have known then that everyone measured it differently, and that no one could measure it better than a young boy full of dreams.

This, then, was Pietro's dream: to die knowing he had done the right thing, that he had not only lived up to his dreams, but provided a good sprouting ground for the dreams of his wife and children. But it seemed the not-knowing would follow him to the grave. The not-knowing was this: Would his grandsons dream of fishing for mountain trout in a stream so pure you could see your ancestors winking at you from under the water? Would one day of such fishing bring peace (and success) to their lives? Or would they follow the paths of automobiles each day, along with thousands of others, which ran along the cloudy and foul-smelling American rivers, and brought them to boxed-up offices full of stale, unbreathable air? Would it even be possible, Pietro thought, that things that had always been held dear, even essential to a sane life, would be considered unimportant by future generations? And all because of the new promised land, a land where life had to be reinvented in order to make people happy: America.

These were cumbersome thoughts for a tired old man who would rather have been sipping a morning espresso with the other *pensionati* of Castello, and letting the past and future of his family find its way without him.

Manny too felt responsible for the direction of his family. When he and Sam returned home from fishing that evening he saw one of Ellen's familiar lists beckoning him to the kitchen table:

Manny —

Jo is at Cory's and needs to be picked up <u>NO LATER</u> than 7. Stop and pick up dry cleaning. Here's the slip. I'll be home around 7:30. Call Linda at work.

There was, of course, no mention of dinner, assuming that he and Sammy were capable of fending for themselves. It was an assumption Manny had grown accustomed to, but one that always seemed to surprise him. He looked up to the kitchen clock. It was seven-ten. The phone rang, and Ellen pulled up the driveway in her off-white sedan.

"Manny? Who was on the phone?"

"I don't know; they hung up."

"Oh. How was fishing?"

Manny and Sam eyed each other, and began laughing.

"The big one got away, didn't it Sammy?"

"Yeah. It did Mom. We're not kidding."

"Then why are you laughing?"

"Because — you should've been there — Dad caught him first and he got away, then I snagged him and Dad got him up with the net. And we were looking for this kid we met who showed us where to fish to show him, but that thing was so strong he bounced up out of the net and got away again! It was awesome."

"Too bad," she sighed. "I was hoping your Dad would put fish on the grill tonight."

Sam stayed quiet a moment, then looked up again at his mother.

"No, it was okay, Mom. I mean, we caught him, right Dad?"

"Absolutely. It was awesome. Maybe Mom will come with us next time."

"What about Jo?" Ellen said quickly, as if she had just entered into the conversation.

"I don't know," Manny said. "We just got home."

"Oh, great. She was supposed to be picked up fifteen minutes ago. And that Sally Eaton is so particular about things like that."

"Screw Sally Eaton," Manny said, much to Sam's delight and surprise. "Maybe if she had a life she wouldn't be worried about things like that."

"Sally Eaton is a neurosurgeon, Manny."

"That doesn't mean she has a *life*, a real one—you know—fishing, meditating, conversing with people you don't know from work. Know what I mean?"

Ellen went blank, then picked up her keys again.

"Okay. I'll get her."

It was that blank look that always got to him: not worried, not reflective, not even concerned. She didn't have it often, but every time he saw it Manny didn't know whether to shake her, snap his fingers, or flee. In any case, he felt he didn't know her then. It was as if a paper cutout had taken her place. "Listen, Ellen," he practiced. "I wasn't kidding when I said Sally Eaton doesn't have a life." He considered what her response might be: "Really. Oh. What?" It wasn't that she was incapable of getting philosophical, just that she saw no point to it. Life was an undulating series of repeatable events which included work, laundry, grocery shopping, and buying shoes for the kids. Why bother with unnecessary mental challenges when every precious random moment should be spent resting, or seeking ways to find rest?

Manny spent the next hour or so walking around the house in Ellen's shoes, trying to see things from her point of view. But everything ended up looking the same. He tried to think of what went on in her head, and the result was a blank. Was there a time when he could see her thoughts, and know her words? Or had that only been an illusion?

When she and Jo came through the doorway Manny was geared to continue his point, but he saw that Ellen's face showed no more interest in the topic, much less in anything else. There was only exhaustion there, a worldly weariness that precluded any possibility of meaningful thought. He decided not to pursue it.

"Hi Dad."

Jo's face appeared and disappeared before his as she passed him on her way to her room, where she would spend her last daylight hours doing homework.

Ellen made herself a tuna sandwich and then a phone call to her sister before declaring the early end of another tired day. She did search Manny out for the obligatory goodnight kiss, and she looked about to say something, but instead yawned and waved her hand as if to say never mind, it wasn't important.

The day finally caught up with Manny, too, and he too decided to end it early.

She was nearly fast asleep, and Manny felt that her very form in the darkness, the way she cuddled up to her pillow and let one hand out over the covers, was becoming routine.

"Hey," he said.

She hummed semiconsciously.

"You asleep?"

"I *was*."

"Never mind then."

"No, no. What then?"

"Nothing in particular."

"I'm really tired tonight honey."

"I wasn't just horny," he said sharply. "I just thought we could talk."

She hummed again.

"You know, above and beyond our regular low maintenance level."

"Then what's wrong?" she asked.

"Do you want to go for a walk?"

She perched on her elbow and looked at him now for the first time.

"Why?"

His answer was a long time coming: "For a change."

"Manny, let's go to sleep and talk in the morning."

She snuggled back in to her falling-asleep position and closed her eyes. The bed shook lightly and she felt Manny's weight being lifted from it.

"Manny?"

"I'm going myself if you don't want to go."

"Stop. Wait. Okay, I'm coming." She turned quickly out of bed and threw on a pair of jeans and a T-shirt. While brushing her hair quickly she noticed that Manny, already dressed, was peering over the side of the bed. "What are you doing?"

"Looking for my shoes."

"Just wear any pair."

He straightened up and looked at her in fear and a sense of betrayal. Surely she must know by now how important it was for him to choose the right pair of shoes.

"I'll wait downstairs," she needled.

"Berkeley's cool at night," he began as they moved away from their house. "I forgot that."

"Mmm."

He looked at her sharply, but she was not focused on him.

"So," she said now, "what?"

"What?"

"You wanted to talk?"

"Not about anything in particular."

"So we're out here walking in the cold for no reason?"

"Bingo!" he shouted. "Okay. See, you don't think this is important. I do."

"Because you think we should talk?"

"Not just. We need to have a little more spontaneity. We need to do things without a reason or a schedule. We need to stop analyzing why we're doing things!" He looked over and saw a look of surprise on her face. His voice had risen steadily as he spoke. "Come on, now, say something," he said.

"Okay," she hesitated. Her breathing had become short. "Let me tell you something now. It's like—sure, we can be spontaneous. We can take off work and go fishing or whatever. But then we still have to come home and do laundry, and take Sammy to a birthday party, and make sure there's food in the house, and — and then go to work the next day and find all the work we didn't get done the day we took off. How can I have a good time when I have all that on my mind?"

For a moment he couldn't answer. Then it struck him:

"That's it, that's it. It's on your mind. Why can't you let things go until you need to think about them?"

"Don't play naïve, Manny. You know there are some things you just can't put on hold. Like the kids, for instance?"

"Ellen, stop treating them like babies."

"I'm not treating them like babies. But they're still living with us, aren't they? Under our protection?"

"Okay. I guess what I want isn't possible."

"What you want—" she paused. "—is to have your cake and eat it too."

He let a few seconds go by for effect.

"It's not a bad thing to want. And even better to work for. Maybe all that matters is the struggle, not the result. If you think you've got something, then you have it. Even if there is a pile of work waiting for you the next day."

"You know..." she said, now softly and calmly, without finishing.

"What?"

"Never mind."

"Come on."

"That's what made me love you. I forget sometimes. It's good to be reminded."

"Do I have to remind you?" He nearly smiled.

"Not always in words, Manny. Not always in words. I'm not that far gone." She touched his arm, and everything they had said evaporated into the stillness. Words hung about them like the fog that had already settled in treetops. He put his arm around her and drew her close, so close that nothing more could be said that might undo them. They walked back this way and closed the door on the conversation-filled trees behind them.

Home was where there was nothing more to be said.

CHAPTER 19

THE NEXT DAY MANNY CAME HOME WITH A CREW CUT.

"Manny. What's gotten into you?" Ellen asked him between phone calls.

"Nothing."

"The hair. Why?"

"I don't know. I just felt like it. It's cool for the summer."

"Summer's almost done. Besides, summers are cool here."

"Okay, okay—have the last word."

"Oh Manny, I didn't mean—"

Before she could finish he was on his way out the door to buy ice cream for himself.

He was beyond bringing her into this. Every now and then in the course of his life he felt the need to redirect his energies, and often this meant modifying his appearance somewhat, in order to announce this new direction to the world. Usually, he meant to discover new territory in his outlook; he meant to make his life new and hopefully better. But the new direction he felt himself taking this evening was an old one, for it led him straight back to his childhood.

Becoming a father was something that came naturally to Manny; he didn't feel he had to work much at it, or to emulate other fathers he'd known (both familial or otherwise). He only relied on the spark in him to make decisions, to know what was right for his kids. But lately that had changed. Lately he had begun reflecting more on why his mother had raised him the way she had, or how his father had influenced him before he had died. And how had his father been raised? What was the driving force behind his grandfather's parental code? Did anyone reflect on such things back than? Or was this the product of having too much time to think about living, instead of just living?

Manny needed to re-inhabit that lost childhood world and see it again from his adult point of view. He needed to learn from everyone who had loved him back then; he needed to walk in each of their shoes.

Almost anything could be found in Manny's car: on the seats, on the floor, tucked into the side pockets or the glove compartment, or dangling from the retracted sun visors. Often, he would throw piles of notes and folders from work onto the front seat next to him, rarely checking to see what lay underneath. Halfway to the ice cream store he noticed the old photograph gleaming at him from the corner of his eye. He ignored it.

But while sitting in the parking lot with his banana split he couldn't help pulling it from the pile. He hadn't looked at it for weeks, maybe months: the picture of his grandmother's family that he had restored.

Pina winked at him first, and he recognized her playful stare watching him as if she had known him on the day the picture was taken. He scanned the rest of the photograph, feeling satisfied at the seamless restoration work he had done. He was especially satisfied seeing Pietro again—the reconstructed eye and lips, the smooth dark suit and perfect crooked tie. Manny wished he could meet him, to see just how accurate his work was.

"Ellen—check this out."

He handed her the picture; a light smile passed over her lips as she spoke:

"Oh Manny. Look how beautiful your grandmother is. And there's your Aunt Mary, and who's—wait a minute. This guy looks like you!"

"Who?"

"Right here, look."

"That's my great-grandfather. I did a number on him, didn't I?"

"What do you mean?"

"He only had one eye when I started, and his tie was half gone, and his—"

"Oh. I see it now."

"Yeah, I really did—"

"No, not that. I mean the resemblance. Something about the eyes, or the lips, or—look at his shoes! They're perfect!"

"He was a shoemaker."

Ellen froze.

"A shoemaker?"

"Yes. A shoemaker. I heard he made some very fine shoes."

"So that's where you get it."

"Get what?"

"Your obsession."

"Oh bullshit. Don't start in on me about that again."

"Okay honey. I know, you can't help it. But it's very interesting—this genetic link."

"I'm going to bed."

From Manny's bedside armchair, where he sat thinking, the photograph lay on a small table, just out of reach. He had been studying it again, and its light sepia nearly glowed by the moonlight that reached it from the window. And as Manny sat there, tired and confused, he saw Pietro rise and take the seat opposite him, all gray and silver shadow.

"Okay, Manny. I tell you something."

Manny nodded, stunned but captivated.

"You think I could sit around and do nothing in my life?" There was that movement in his eyes now, that thing that was missing from the photograph. "I did. When I was a boy."

"And then?" Manny said. "That's where I am now."

97

Pietro took a long time to answer. A smile crossed his lips.

"You think, you think. And then time passes and you don't think anymore. You are busy, like everybody else. You are just living."

"I know. I'm busy too."

"Listen, Manlio. When I came to America I knew everything. But now I know I learned something there. I learned that even if you don't like getting up early in the morning to go to work you will forget about it after a while. And I learned that if you are a little bit hungry or tired while you're working, and you just keep working, then you will forget that you were hungry or tired. And if you are angry with your wife and children so that it is burning you inside then you will love them just as much, so that you will never know if that burn is anger or love. And pretty soon, yes even sooner that you think, all that matters is that burn. Because everything around you becomes like a dream — the beautiful hills and rivers you loved as a child become a dream. The sun and rain and snow are a dream. The smoky sky and oily streets are a dream. All you are left with is the look you find in everyone's eyes, the same look. The same burn. It is there, Manlio. It is what drew you to our photograph."

"I know," Manlio quietly said. "I think I know what you mean. I think I remember that feeling. It might even come back to me at times. But it's never there all the time. Why —"

"Things are changing for you the way they changed for me, Manlio. You are starting something new. I have no advice for you, as no one had for me."

"Is this change for the good?"

"Who can know? Not even the dead can tell you this. All we can do is give comfort to your journey. You are learning something I will never know about, something that will take your whole life to learn. I know what it means to learn, even the pain of being confused, the giving up and lost hope. These are the rules of living...."

Manny didn't know how long he had been listening. He looked over to the bed and found Ellen sleeping there; he hadn't even heard her come in. Then he looked back to the chair. He thought at first that Pietro had disappeared, but he was still there, rocking slowly, back and forth in the silver moonlight. And just as Manny was about to speak again Pietro winked at him, resuming his familiar smirk and place in the photograph.

Pietro's great-grandson dropped his head into his hands. The fog had arrived, gradually fading out the moonlight and casting a pall over the room.

Pina noticed the gradual changes in her father's health, and wondered if he would make it to see her son become a man. She noted too the slow changes in his face, the way everything fell away from his eyes and left an imprint of his life there. As a mature woman of forty-one she was beginning to recognize more and more of that life and equating it with her own. When she looked into the mirror at night, she could see the future looking back at her; she could see her father's old eyes in hers. But she resisted becoming him, because to become him would mean betraying who she was. Her eyes had spent a childhood and adolescence in Castel di Sangro and seen a sharp turn on the road to adulthood when she was brought to America, as in a dream. Her father's dreamlife was different; her father's had arrived in middle age, after the lines in his face had been set.

And yet his eyes did stare back at her, even if they were not his eyes. Surprisingly, this was both a shock and a relief to her. The shock was that she could be so firmly tied to him, and the relief was that they had shared a terrible and exciting dream.

"Almerinda!"

"She's not here," Pina replied.

"Almerinda!"

"*Babbo, zitto! Non ci sta.* She went to look after Zia Teresa."

"Almerinda! Where is she?"

"What do you want?" Pina shouted.

"I want breakfast. Two soft-boiled eggs. Toast. Orange juice and coffee. Can you make eggs, Pina?"

Pina rolled her eyes. Pietro refocused on them. Neither looked away first.

"Five minutes," she said. "Don't bother me until then."

He opened his mouth as if to speak, but all that came was a grunt. His face stayed like that for a moment in a state of confusion, uncertain of its role. This trance was broken by the kitchen door handle's turning, and the light shove that opened the door.

"Mamma," Pina said. "Babbo's driving me nuts."

Almerinda's face was also tired, and her eyes less vibrant than her aging husband's, but they could still draw attention.

"Let it go. I'll finish."

Pietro gathered his remaining energy to seat himself at the table. Now that Almerinda was there he needn't give further instruction. Pina left the kitchen without a word, though her presence was still felt after she'd gone. She and Jim would spend this Saturday morning packing for the move to their new home, a house similar to her parents', on the next block. Pietro and Almerinda would be left to their morning routine, with a slight variation today. Almerinda had an announcement to make:

"Teresa's coming to live with us."

Pietro felt a slight sensation in his head, a registering of something unpleasant.

"She'll be here day after tomorrow. I'm setting her up in Pina's and Jim's room."

At this point his silence was premeditated. He breathed deeply and asked for more coffee.

"She'll need a little help getting up and down the stairs."

"Not from me."

"*Santa Lucia*. And what if you should need help someday? And I say, not from me?"

His eyes lifted, and filled with youthful vigor.

"You're my wife. She's not."

The day after Pina and Jim moved out and Almerinda's sister moved in a small fire broke out in the house. It started in Teresa's room, and was luckily contained there by Almerinda, who took a bucket from the closet, filled it with water, and mindlessly threw it on the flaming bedspread. Teresa was nowhere to be found.

When Pietro came through the kitchen door from his morning garden check he heard the water dripping from the ceiling onto the Formica table. At first he just stood and watched, as if it were an apparition that would soon be gone. But his eyes were not so old as to fool him: the water was real, plaster melted away from the ceiling, and a wide brown ring was growing there.

"*Porco Giuda*," he said, still unable to move.

Almerinda came down with the bucket still in hand, wiping the other on her housedress. She noted the ceiling (but not Pietro) and mumbled to herself: "Eh, too bad." Then, having set the bucket on the table and gone for a dishtowel to wipe up stray drops, she said to him: "Well, what are you going to do about it?"

Pietro seated himself at the sopping table and motioned for his coffee.

"Damn house. Call the plumber. That's what I'll do. Where's the telephone?"

"Same place it was yesterday," she answered. "But the plumber has nothing to do with this."

"I'm tired of fixing every damn thing in this house. I'm calling the plumber, just-so, that's all…"

"Listen, Pietro—" Almerinda stopped when she heard the front door open. In came Teresa, who had been rocking herself into oblivion on the front porch.

"*Buon giorno, buon giorno.* What a nice day it is, Almerinda. No?"

"*Buon giorno,* Teresa."

She took a seat across from Pietro, whose eyes were fixed on the ceiling. The last drops hung there undecidedly. Almerinda sat between them, and looked at Teresa directly:

"Teresa, were you smoking cigarettes?"

"Cigarettes? No, of course not. Dirty habit."

"Then why was your bed on fire this morning?"

"What?" Pietro awakened.

"On fire?" Teresa whispered. Then slowly to herself: "On *fire.* Let me think. All I did was say my morning prayers. I lit my candle and started with my devotions to the Virgin. Then, then… Can I remember? I didn't want to wake you, Almerinda, so I went to relieve myself and then made it down the stairs—by myself—"

Pietro's right hand came down so hard on the table that the salt and pepper shakers flew up and landed as all three watched. "This is why I—"

"Quiet!" said Almerinda. "Teresa, do you light a candle every morning when you pray?"

Teresa looked back at her in utter dismay.

"Of course. Because I can't make it to church. By myself, that is."

"I'll get a nice votive candle for you, Teresa, with a lid and a stand that doesn't move."

Pietro rose and said semiaudibly: "I'll take that stand, candle, and damned lid and smash them into a thousand little pieces."

"Pay no attention to him," Almerinda said. "He's like that."

A final drop fell from the ceiling and into the bucket. It startled the women, but Pietro didn't seem to hear. He took the bucket, emptied it into the sink, and left it there for his wife to tuck away into one of those mysterious places where such things ended up.

Almerinda went to the Catholic store that afternoon to buy Teresa's votive candle; it flickered in its wrought iron stand all night and was there for Teresa the next morning as she blessed herself and began her morning prayers.

The faded brown ring on the kitchen ceiling remained and was never mentioned again.

CHAPTER 20

MANNY AWAKENED FROM HIS LESS-THAN-PERFECT sleep to find that Ellen was gone. His dim recollection of her shadow lying there was replaced by the bright white sheet lying flatly in wide wrinkles. He stared at the sheet, hoping for a clue to her whereabouts, but finally decided to put on his robe and head downstairs.

There was no smell of coffee, but a vague lingering of burnt toast and raw egg. Manny felt, as he approached the kitchen, that he would be spending this Saturday only half-awakened, but when he looked up his heart landed in his mouth, and blood rushed to his face. The room was a mess. Eggshells bled onto the counter; measuring cups of every capacity lay in all directions; a bag of flour spilled onto the floor; a warming carton of milk sat on the stove; the spice cabinet hung open, with several of its tins and jars transferred to various lengths of the counter, along with a bag of walnuts and two sets of measuring spoons. On the table, which was splattered with syrup and melted butter, sat three used plates, a pile of sticky paper napkins, stray forks, and half-emptied glasses of cola. In a far corner, just beside the microwave, a round waffle iron smoked, closed. Manny looked up again, this time to heaven, but all he found there was a clock that read 9:45.

"Ellen!"

It came quickly from his mouth, unexpectedly. In the next second, he realized she wasn't home, that he had called her out of habit, but his confusion grew deeper when he saw her standing in the doorway, the morning light pouring in around her.

"What the hell happened here?" she asked. She grew still under Manny's stare.

"I sure didn't do it," he said.

The answer passed simultaneously behind their eyes, and each felt palpitations of the heart at the thought of Jo following in her father's footsteps.

"She must have had someone over for breakfast," Ellen mumbled.

"Sam?" Manny said.

"He's still sleeping. Let's see—one, two, three plates. Hmm. Did she say she was off to somewhere this morning?"

"I didn't talk to her last night," he said.

"Neither did I."

Another realization passed between them, creating a gust of cold wind that blew about the kitchen. Ellen tried to ignore it, but Manny felt he couldn't. He waited for her to say something, but she shifted her attention to the dishes that needed tidying up.

The cold air was replaced by the stark clanking of dishes, and occasional quiet.

But Ellen, he thought, *why don't we talk to our daughter? Why don't we know where she is? Why didn't we know she wanted to learn how to cook?* Ellen's words reached him as if through a telescope:

"Why don't you show her how to do this next time? You're better at it than I am. I mean, I can measure things out and mix them together like a good scientist, but you're the creative one, Manny. She needs that."

"Why does she need everything from me?"

"Everything? All right, she doesn't need everything from you. She *has* everything from you. She's just like you Manny. So you can reach her better than I can."

"Bull."

"That's what she'd say."

He had begun clearing off the table and putting things away.

"I think you don't want to deal with it."

"What do you mean? I'm dealing with it by telling you to deal with it." She laughed. It both tickled and distracted him. It seemed too complicated a time to be laughing. Years, even months ago he would have chuckled with her. But now there was only a little void inside him where the laughter should have been. He

105

answered her with a mumble, surprising even himself with his bluntness:

"I won't be the only one to deal with problems in this house."

It was met with an overly quick response.

"What's the matter with you, Manny? You've never talked to me like that before."

"I'm just being honest. I'm letting you know how I feel. I'd expect you to do the same." He paused. "Remember?"

But nothing more could be said; Jo came crashing into the room and filled it again with vitality and an adolescent warmth.

"Sweetheart," Ellen began, "why didn't you ask your father to help you with these? They might have turned out better."

"What do you mean? They were great. Ask Sammy."

"But you might have cleaned up.

"Dad doesn't clean up when he cooks."

"I do too," Manny shot.

"Not right away. Look, I came back to do it now. Go ahead, leave. I'll do it all."

"No, no, we've already started —" Ellen began.

"Goodbye, Mom!" Jo looked squarely at her mother with the exact look that Ellen had seen once in an old photograph of Manny's grandmother. It nearly sent her the chills.

Manny shrugged and left the room. Ellen soon followed him and touched him on the shoulder the way she sometimes did, sending him into remission of whatever thoughts he was having and replacing them with nothing but her.

"Manny, let's go out for breakfast."

Jim had promised a million times to have a look at Pietro's temperamental car, but when the day arrived that they were to visit Giancarlo and his family in Vandergrift it sat dead still in the garage. Nothing on Earth, it seemed, could make it go.

Almerinda voiced her unsolicited advice once again:

"You should have taken it to a mechanic from the start."

"And how to take it there?" Pietro quipped. "With wings?"

Within a couple of hours they were on a city bus, and their little journey had begun.

Neither of them could remember the last time they had been together on even the slightest adventure, like this one. It was enough to make them both feel a little uncomfortable, as if they were being censored somehow for this extraordinary, reckless action.

For the first ten minutes they didn't speak, which was nothing new. They seldom spoke these days unless it was necessary. But it was the change of scenery, and the changing scenery, that stirred them and brought old feelings back to them. Pietro began to wonder why they had nothing to talk about, while Almerinda tried earnestly to provide an opening remark.

"A nice cloud over there," Pietro finally said.

"Where?"

"There."

"Where?"

"See it? Right over that little hill."

"Which hill?"

"Never mind."

"What?"

"Never mind."

The bus driver shifted down in anticipation of the changing traffic light, throwing them both a little forward, like a pair of nodding parrots. At the light a stillness seemed to overcome everyone on the bus. Pietro felt himself holding his breath until he finally blurted out —

"Why are we waiting? Nobody coming the other way."

The driver looked back at him, shrugged, and pulled out through the intersection. The light had not yet changed back to green. Pietro and Almerinda felt the bus's familiar hum again, as well as every pothole, large and small, knocking them about. Pietro's left hand flew up at one point and came down on Almerinda's lap. She herself flew a couple of inches into the air, brushing her skirt (and Pietro's hand off) as she came down. Pietro responded by waiting for the next big pothole so he could slip his hand under her bottom as she flew up again. He even thought of squeezing it, but before he could carry out his plan, he nearly fell off the seat: the driver had swerved to miss hitting a stray dog. Almerinda grabbed her husband's arm in a way she hadn't for years, holding onto it as if it offered her something more than what was needed to prevent her from falling off too.

After they had settled there came the realization to both of them that they hadn't touched each other for quite some time until now. Pietro, for one, felt his balance off-center because of it. And Almerinda felt herself trying to ignore the feelings it had resurrected inside her.

"Do you think Giancarlo will have a good lunch waiting for us?" Pietro asked.

"Of course. What else?"

"He can be full of shit sometimes."

Almerinda turned her head in mock astonishment: "What?"

"You heard me well."

"Yes. He can be full of shit. And his wife too."

This time Pietro turned his head; he was not accustomed to hearing her talk like that. Pina, yes, but not Almerinda. It both frightened and pleased him. He noticed she was smiling.

"So why are we going?" he said.

She shrugged. "What else? Just-so, that's all."

Pietro's eyebrow went up. It was the first time she had used his pet phrase. He took her hand and pressed it as she watched the hills go by from the window.

Pina stopped by her mother's the next day to pick up the dress she was going to alter. Almerinda's eyes could no longer guide her hand to thread the needle, and Pina's work as a seamstress at St. Francis Hospital had sharpened her skills well beyond what her mother's had been. She often stopped on the way home from work to visit her parents, and she could not remember a time when they were not there to greet her. Almerinda would be making dinner, and Pietro would be playing with the radio, or poking around in the garden. The door would be open and Pina would walk right in, shouting her loud, resonant, "*Mamma!*"

But today the door was jammed; she pushed it hard twice and still it would not open. She tried peeking in through the long windows on either side of the door, though they were clouded by lace curtains on the inside. Nothing moved inside the house as far as she could see. Finally she threw her hands up and headed home to Jim, cursing the locked door and the time it had made her lose.

He had not waited for her but started boiling water for the pasta and warming the sauce, saying nothing as she walked into the kitchen.

"Not enough water," she said.

"Enough for me," he replied. "Who knows when you come home."

She sighed with a smile, and immediately shot back—

"You know what to do here—except for the water."

"Okay. Tell me. Where were you?"

"I stopped at Mamma's but nobody was home."

"Not even Zia Teresa?"

"No."

"Funny," he said.

"Just-so, that's all," she concluded, taking over the dinner preparations and checking to see that their son had finished his homework.

As they were having their coffee Zia Teresa called; she sounded nearly out of breath with fear and excitement. She had come home from visiting her friend Ange and found neither Almerinda nor Pietro there to help her with the steps. Upon calling their names loudly she found no response. It wasn't until after she had relieved herself and warmed a plate of *maccherone* with butter for dinner that the phone rang. It was Pietro, who made no pretense about having to endure a conversation with her about an unavoidable matter.

He began by reminding Teresa about the trip he and Almerinda had made to Giancarlo's, to which Teresa replied that she did not recall them ever telling her about the trip, that they never told her much at all, *at all*, and that her status in the house was one step above servant. Pietro, silent during this monologue, continued: "In fact your sister has fallen and sprained her wrist. We stayed the night to see if she would recover." And then he added after a pointedly long pause: "She was drunk."

"Drunk? What do you mean?"

"I mean, Teresa, that she was drunk. On wine, as supplied by the good Signor Purtelli. A fine vintage it was, too."

Pietro's last words brought that pleasant taste back to his mouth, and he was about to give his sister-in-law every detail of the evening, right up to Almerinda's fateful turn, when he heard the receiver click and the phone go dead.

And so Teresa related to Pina how one of her father's insensitive friends had driven her poor mother over the brink of incivility and that as a result of her unpardonable behavior she had been the victim of a tragic accident.

"She fell?" Pina inquired.

"On her wrist, *la poverina*," Teresa said.

"And you're telling me what? That Signor Purtelli gave her a little bit of wine?"

"More than a little bit, *cara Pina*."

"Good. She needed that."

"What? How do you know?" Teresa asked innocently.

"Because she always needs that. She's too serious."

"Pina! Shame, shame, shame. Telling me your mother needs to get drunk. What's the limit with you? This is from your father."

"Zia Teresa, tell me, when can we expect them home?"

"Tomorrow."

"All right, then I'll be stopping by after work to make them dinner. Thank you, Zi-zi. *Buona notte.*"

Jim's eyes widened. Pina anticipated his reaction and stepped right in with her usual timing:

"Of course we can all eat there together. At six o'clock."

He nodded lightly while looking down at the plate of *biscotti* she had set in the middle of the table. No other topic of discussion could divert his attention now.

CHAPTER 21

THEY COULDN'T DECIDE WHERE TO SIT. The restaurant, though small, offered them too many choices: near the window, along the wall, back in the corner. They settled on a table that put them directly in the center. As soon as they sat down, though, they felt they had made a mistake, for now they were the center of everyone's attention.

Ellen hummed and looked around the room, but Manny kept his eyes on her.

"What?" she said.

"Nothing in particular. I was just blanking out again."

"Is everything okay?"

"I don't know. What do you mean by that?"

"I mean, are you happy?"

He took a while to answer, and by this she knew the answer was anything but yes.

"Now what does that mean?" he said to himself. But she heard.

"I think something's bothering you. Otherwise, you would have ordered by now."

He looked up and smiled faintly. She did know something about him.

"So what do you think about our lives?" he finally said.

"What do you mean by that?"

"I guess neither of us know what we mean today. It's pretty general, really. Do you think our family's okay—I mean, the way we live?"

"As opposed to what?"

Her expression was exactly like that of a confused child's, he thought. But then she caught herself, and continued:

112

"My friend Ginny, you know her, don't you? She does it all alone. She has two kids, works full time, takes them to baseball games, the whole bit. And they seem completely normal to me."

"What's normal? As crazy as everyone else?"

"We're not crazy, Manny. Come on now. You're making me feel bad."

"I'm not afraid to feel bad. Why are you? It's better than not feeling at all."

Now he had done it, cut to the bone with one of his bullseye remarks. Sometimes they surprised even him. He couldn't tell whether she'd laugh or cry next.

"Listen Ellen, I'm just thinking out loud. Like you do sometimes. Right? I'm just wondering what things were like in the old days, when everyone had just one job to do instead of everyone having every job to do, like it is today."

"It's not that bad, Manny."

"I don't know if it's bad or not, I just want to know whether it's right."

"I—"

"Imagine this." He was becoming animated. "Imagine the whole family getting up at the same time to have breakfast."

"Oh God. Leave It to Beaver."

"Come on. Now just try to use your imagination. Forget that things were ever that black-and-white on TV. In real life, yes, there was a time when people ate breakfast together. But I'm not talking about going back in time. I'm talking about imagining something new. What's wrong with everyone being on the same schedule? Say the kids went to school from seven to one, and then we all came home to prepare and eat a meal together. Then you and I did homework with them, after a nap of course. Every day. Instead of staring at a computer screen with a brain full of sleep-deprived afternoon mush."

"I can't imagine it. And what about the rest of the day?"

"I don't know. Anything—reading, playing, fixing things, maybe some TV."

"That's what we do now!"

"But we're not together," he said.

"And what's the difference? If you're reading a book, it doesn't matter if someone else is in the house or not."

"It's a complete lack of rigid schedule I'm talking about. A lot of quality free-association time. A lot."

"Manny, that's never been the case, all through history."

"So what. Before this century it was never the case that everyone could learn to read and write. Now we are more sophisticated as a whole, and there's no reason why we shouldn't have more creative time, not less of it. Otherwise, we'll get stuck in the Dark Ages, Part Two. A lot of busy rats running around filling up schedules we've arbitrarily created for ourselves."

She considered what he'd said for a moment, then spoke: "What is this schedule you keep talking about?"

His mouth opened but nothing came out. Then his eyebrows knitted downwards, and he shook his head. "*What?* You don't feel that every second of your day is planned?"

"Well, yes. But that's just the way it is right now. Things will be different when we're older. Listen, Manny, you're going through a rough time now. Things aren't as bad as you think."

"Like I said. I'm not thinking about bad or good—that can change by the minute. I'm talking about what's *right*."

"I don't know what that means either. I suppose that can change too, depending on the times. Was it right that my great-grandmother had twelve kids?"

"I don't know," he said. "But it was definitely right that they all learned how to sing. And you didn't hear any of them complaining about money. That seems right to me—I guess it's the same as having priorities. What kind of priorities do I have? To get through a day in one piece, and hope I won't have to think about the next until it comes?"

"Why not?" she answered. "Live each day to its fullest."

"But not with a dagger at your throat. That's not living. It's coercion."

"I see," she said lightly, as if cueing him in to the fact that she was throwing in the towel on this conversation. "So what do you want to do about it?"

"I was hoping you'd say 'we'."

"Mmm."

"But I'm going to start cultivating the art of saying no."

"No to what?"

"No to anything or anyone. I'm going to get things in balance. If anything's tipping my life too much in one direction, I'll just put a stop to it. That's the only way to do it. And if everyone did it, no one would be out of balance and things in general would work better."

"I didn't know I was married to an idealist."

"How about *realist*?"

"Manny."

"What?"

"Don't say no to me, okay?"

Their eyes locked. He had not excluded her from this new outlook. This was unfair.

"Not for anything important, like bedtime activities," he answered.

That got her to smile; the rest, he thought, would be left to her imagination.

Manny thought it necessary to buy a new pair of shoes that afternoon: the weather was changing, and everything appeared to him in a new light. The way his feet touched the earth needed attention, for that had changed too.

It was a day that was neither cool nor hot, windy nor still, and the sun shone unevenly, as if its light were being filtered through an unfamiliar medium. Manny felt not oppressed but refreshened by this day. But the question he carried with him was: What kind of shoes to buy? Nothing he had would have matched his mood. Should they be sleek black sneakers, or soft brown loafers? It might be best to get them both. Then he could change shoes all day, and let his feet feel something of the day's complexity.

The first thing he did, after putting on the new sneakers, was drive to one of his favorite lookouts in the Berkeley hills. On the way up the eucalyptus-lined road he slowed as he remembered that Sammy's soccer game was at one o'clock. Manny was not formally one of the coaches, but he had lent himself to the role more often than not, in the absence of others. He regained speed while realizing that there was still time for his walk. It would take him about twenty minutes to drive back home, and another ten to take Sammy to the field. The games were normally one and a half hours long. If the weather were damp, they'd break earlier, ten minutes at most, but that happened rarely. Maybe he could just drop Sammy off and hope one of the other parents would bring him home.

Manny considered every possibility for tailoring his schedule to fit that soccer game in. Only after he had come up with some comfortable solution did he stop to wonder why he hadn't thought of another one: call Ellen and have her take Sammy to the game.

A walk in the fog, he thought, would do him good. He would be able to see little but his next step. As he parked the car he remembered (having forgotten in the last minute) to call Ellen about the game. He wasn't expecting any particular response from her, but was surprised when she gladly accepted the obligation, adding that he should take his time and do "whatever he needed to do." He was not sure whether to feel relieved or betrayed by the hidden condescension. It was only a walk.

Wind moved along the dried grasses and wild anise, forming patterns where they swayed together and apart. It looked to Manny as if the slope were conversing with itself and inviting him into the conversation. The fog was coming in quickly, distorting the landscape into fragments that lacked connection or perspective. Manny's first step on the path felt soft on his feet; the black sneakers with their soothing light leather carried him forward gently and surely, like an inflated raft over swift water. He began running, and the dark sneakers turned white. His body lightened, and his legs sprang from the ground as if they could never feel fatigue. The mowed summer field was the distance of his boyhood spreading infinitely around him, the freedom of his future. His laced canvas sneakers were a symbol of this. He kept them safely under his bed when he wasn't wearing them, had his mother buy new laces for them, wiped mud from them after playing in the rain.

But his legs stopped, and he began to feel their weight. The canvas sneakers turned to hard brown loafers, and life became serious. The steps he took now were not just his own; they were matched by others. Everyone opened the same books, answered the same questions. Even their shoes looked like his—a fact he couldn't bear, because he knew even then that no one's shoes could feel like his, could give him comfort and guidance the way his did. A few long years went by and he found that he was allowed to choose what to wear on his own, that he could find the shoes that set him rightly apart from the others. He felt then that he was on his way again—not the careless way he'd traveled as a child, but one that hinted of danger, awareness, and exhilaration. It kept him going, wearing out one pair of shoes after another,

117

until the day he took his shoes off, and spent a summer going barefoot. That was the summer before he went to college.

Now his life had taken quite a turn, and his feet would never be the same, for he found them wandering almost anywhere. He went dancing, hiking, and running; found himself traversing whole cities, finding ways that were all but hidden from others, ways that led him to new discoveries about the world and himself. In fact, shoes became more important for him than ever, because never before had he used his feet so exhaustively.

Until he graduated and began to work. In this new kind of exhaustion, he never stopped to look at his shoes, or bother about what kind they were, because there seemed to be little variation in the kind of shoes that were permitted in the working environment. During the first couple of years, he actually wore holes in his shoes, and casually replaced them with clones, having completely forgotten the care he had once taken in choosing his footwear. But then, one smug day, he cast his shoes off under his desk and curled his toes onto one another in an act of corporate defiance. He looked to the window and focused on nothing, for there was the future hung distantly and unattainably before him, a parade of new shoes without owners waiting, waiting...

Life had finally come around. He slipped his black wing tips back on and headed for the nearest shoe shop. When he returned to the office one hour later his colleagues noticed the fresh glow in his expression before gasping in horror at the site of his new, mottled snakeskin boots. The following day he wore light brown suedes, and on Friday he showed up in high-top sneakers. This individuality, however, did not reveal itself in the rest of his clothing. No one knew quite what to say about this, so most said nothing. At an important client meeting that Friday Manny's supervisor took great care to see that everyone remained seated around the long table until he had escorted their clients back to the elevator. Manny said little at the meeting, but wore a gentle, lambent smile that was the envy of everyone present.

Because his path through life was now more clearly marked, Manny began to feel more aware of it, and more responsible for the choices he made along the way. He no longer felt the heat of indecision rising in his breast. Often he came early to the office, and used that time to let design problems solve themselves. He would look down at his oxblood loafers or Italian ankle boots and realize that he had something to offer this world. And it would come.

The fog had lifted and burned away as surely as it had come, leaving Manny's footprints to be lighted by the strong sun of late afternoon. He had walked far into the fog, and now it was gone, leaving him exposed to the hard-edged present. His daydream, along with his hike, had come to an end. But far from being deposited into the glaring world of his frantic day-life, he found himself in the middle of a quiet field where wild herbs released their complicated scents to him. He almost felt that he needed a new pair of shoes for the hike back to his car, so renewed and novel did he feel. Even the path he had worn would be different going back: his own footprints would seem unfamiliar, uncreated.

CHAPTER 22

PIETRO LIFTED THE SHOES FROM THEIR BOX, unwrapped them from their brown paper, turned them over in his hands, and dropped them onto the floor.

"Almerinda!"

Though she did answer him (rather softly from the next room) he called her name again, and again, until she appeared before him, wiping her hands on her apron.

"What are these?"

"New shoes."

"New shoes. And who made these new shoes?"

She took up the box, turned it around, and pretended to read: "*Koffaman.*"

"Tell Signor Koffaman that I wouldn't use these to shovel chicken shit."

"Signor Koffaman makes a lot of things. He made our dining room and the stove I use to make your dinner every day. Everything he makes is good, and no one in this world ever has a problem wearing his shoes."

"If there are a thousand asses running in the streets there is no need to add one more. Where are my good shoes?"

"You don't have good shoes."

"Where are my shoes!"

She pointed to the hall closet on her way back to the kitchen, adding in her unfeeling voice: "We are in America. We wear American shoes."

He pretended not to hear her as he went to find the shoes; they lay directly in front of him after he opened the closet door, like old friends waiting to be noticed again. As he picked one up the sole fell out, and he saw that half the stitching was gone. His next impulse was a mixed one: call Almerinda, find his tools, cut new leather. All future action fused in his mind and left him uncontrollably indecisive, as if there were no distinction between things that had happened and things that might happen. He turned, felt lost for a moment, and headed for the front door, still holding the dilapidated shoe. On his feet were a pair of soft corduroy slippers.

The street was empty this Saturday morning; the air was cool but warming quickly from a steady sun. Pietro looked up, closed his eyes, then let their gaze fall back to the ground. He needed to walk long to Signor Toschi's leather shop, passing his uncle's café, the bridge at Via Bianca, and the gypsy women on his way. Signor Toschi would have a cup of espresso waiting for him, and they would sit and talk about anything but shoes until Almerinda walked by with her mother on the way to the open market. Then Pietro would excuse himself and follow them discreetly, rehearsing opening lines to make her acquaintance. Once his shoulder strap broke and allowed his new leather pieces to unravel on the dusty road, drawing the attention of everyone, it seemed, but her.

He has walked this route a hundred times, and his shoes have never failed to make the walk more comfortable. But today his feet ache, and there is little or no support for them. They are moving, and the ache is moving with them, even affecting his legs, his chest, his hands. But he will not be able to repair this shoe until he buys good leather from his friend Signor Toschi. He thinks this sun will make his aches go away, he wishes it, but his wish is interrupted by a loud voice coming from a man who doesn't speak Italian.

"Hey Grandpap, want a lift?"

It is best not to answer foreigners; their shoes are not good, and whoever does not take care of his feet will never find his way in life, or be trustworthy. It is always best to keep walking, walking away from trouble and into one's destiny.

So he walked, walked, until the scenery became unfamiliar. Had he passed Toschi's leather shop? Had Almerinda already passed by with her mother, leaving him now alone, on a solitary path, without the materials he needed to prepare his feet for another step?

CHAPTER 23

THE DOOR WAS OPEN, BRINGING THE WARM AIR of late afternoon into the cool house. Manny walked in slowly, feeling the warmth and stillness enveloping him as he wondered why this sudden gift of quiet had been offered to him.

"Ellen?"

He walked from one room to the next, back to the kitchen and to the front of the house again. It was not like her not to answer him, so he didn't call her name again, but went upstairs to change his shoes. He stopped in the bathroom to wash his face and hands and saw that her toothbrush was missing. Now a puff of wind came up the back of his throat. He checked the small shelf where she kept some of her make-up; it too was gone. He breathed deeply and headed for their bedroom, tripping over a walkie-talkie that lay in the middle of the hallway. The first thing he saw in the room was her slippers. She had not taken her slippers. But his shoes were there, the ones he wanted, or the ones he had wanted a minute ago. For now, he just sat on the edge of the bed with his head in his hands, wondering what to do next. He kicked off his new black sneakers and did not feel like putting on any other shoes, for there were none that fit his mood. His feet fell flat and immobile on the floor, feeling naked, and unadorned.

Nothing could have moved him from that spot. Nothing could have entered his empty mind, nor the cool rooms of his heart. Then a hand touched his shoulder, and a voice spoke—

"Manny? What are you doing?"

He turned fast enough to send him whirling through space, but the sight of her lying deeply under the white covers stopped him cold. A flood of euphoria mixed with pain and fear ran over him, filling up everything that had been empty in an instant.

"Ellen? I thought you—"

"What?"

"I thought…I don't know. I think I'm crazy."

"I know you are."

"What are you doing up here?"

"Taking a nap. I've been cleaning and running around all day. But I feel pretty good now."

"So do I."

He fell over her and let the weight of the day slip out of him. *Where am I?* he thought. *How could everything have changed so? How do I receive this day's gift; what do I do to return it?* It seemed that all that was good was in place for him again, spontaneous, and outside of his control. And now, before he could think about it, they were making love, kissing like adolescents who were just discovering the depths to which they could go.

It seemed that the moment Manny and Ellen came down the stairs Sammy burst in through the front door and Jo slammed open the one in back. The house had been transformed in an instant from calm to near calamity.

Sammy flew past them on his way up the stairs, and Jo hung around in the kitchen banging cupboard doors in her search for a late snack. Ellen and Manny instinctively headed for the kitchen too, both feeling surprised that they had thought of the same thing.

"What should we have?" Manny said.

"I have some chicken breast."

"Screw chicken breasts. How about, well okay, we can have the chicken, but how about a stir-fry?"

"Okay."

"Don't put celery in, Dad. It's gross," Jo added.

"All right. Then why don't you cut up the vegetables?" he said.

"I don't like carrots!" Sammy shouted from the stairs (coming back down now). "Put in some of those white crunchy things."

"They're called water chestnuts, bonehead."

"Now Jo—you didn't always know everything," Ellen said.

Sammy walked past Jo and kicked her in the knee, but Jo was too concentrated on her vegetable cutting effort to respond. Rolling her eyes and shaking her head was enough. Ellen threw in a few things of her own—snow peas and asparagus—while Manny created the marinade. Within an hour they were eating, each pleased in a different way by the combination of colors and flavors that had resulted. A few minutes had passed before anyone became aware of the silence, a silence which encouraged Jo to remember that she had to write a book report for Monday on a book she hadn't bought yet.

"Dad, can you take me to Barnes and Noble after dinner?"

"How about tomorrow; I think we should all relax tonight."

"I kinda need to go tonight."

"Why?" Ellen interjected.

"Because I just remembered I have to read *A Farewell to Arms* and write a report on it for Monday."

Manny looked up, then down to his plate again—

"Get an extension."

"I can't."

"Why not?"

"Because I got one last time and Mister Rainey says if I'm late again I'll get an F."

"Then maybe you'll learn not to wait until the last minute."

"Okay! Mom, can you take me?"

"I guess so."

"Wait a minute," Manny said. "She has to learn to take care of these things herself—"

"All right! I'll walk there myself. Don't worry about it. I'm sorry to be an inconvenience to you!" She was shouting and beginning to show tears. Ellen called after her as she left the kitchen and stomped up the stairs to her room. After a minute or so of banging doors and piercing ululations she came down again, heading for the front door. Manny stood up at once and called out:

"You are NOT ALLOWED to walk down to that store at this hour." His voice was louder than they'd ever heard it; his words were slow and distinct, and enough to set everyone trembling, including Jo. When she turned around and saw the wild look in his eyes she headed back up the stairs and gave her bedroom door one good last slam. Manny turned back to the kitchen, where Ellen too was tearing up, and Sammy was nowhere to be found.

He sat down and exhaled, aware now that he had been partly holding his breath. Ellen wiped her eyes with her hands as he tried to voice a dozen meaningless phrases, but none came out.

"Where's Sammy?" he finally asked. She shrugged once and shook her head —

"I don't know. Probably out back."

"I'll clean up," he said, as he began to gather the dishes.

"I'm going upstairs to read a little before I go to bed. Manny, maybe you should —"

"Yeah, I'll go get the book after I'm done."

He set the Barnes and Noble bag on the kitchen table at dawn, along with a note that he could be found at his office: he had awakened with an idea and wanted to be alone with it there. No one else would be around so early on a Sunday morning. By the time he found himself at his desk and turned his chair to face the giant office window the sky over Berkeley was filling with rosy light. He quietly slipped off his shoes, raised his feet to rest on the window ledge, and forgot why he had come.

For the first time in months Manny was not afraid. He was not afraid of seeing that he had no direction. In fact, he rather liked it, because it meant that his life was limitless. Slowly he had come to see that certainty in all things makes one feel too mortal. When

all the cards are drawn there is nothing left to do but turn them
in. He preferred now to see them stacked mysteriously in their
deck, the same deck his father had drawn from; and his grandfather, and great-grandfather. And instead of feeling that he had
done little in his life he began to reflect on his accomplishments.
At once they flooded over him: the hillock of papers he'd written
for school, the reams of sketches and stacks of canvases painted,
the meals he'd created and original conversations he'd had, his
intimacies, yards he'd transformed, his children, his marriage. He
thought deeply about his history, and where his family had come
from. He was no longer feeling blindly alone, for he felt they were
feeling with him now — he was part of an undying chain of uncertainty, a chain his very life was helping to forge, but whose design
he would never know.

The sun had risen over the hills; its light showered the bay.
He felt lucky to see it from his twentieth-story window, when others were probably only waking from their playful Saturdays to a
quieter day of submission to thoughts of how far they too had
come in their short lives. Maybe it was only right that he should
join them, instead of condescending to their inferior perspective.

Within the hour two more people had come to the office. At
first everyone worked quietly alone, then they began to visit one
another for conversation and advice. Manny's project began to
breathe, and soon all other considerations left him as it developed
into something within his reach, something that both challenged
and comforted him as he grappled with it and felt its life renewing
his.

After Nonno Fiorentino died Pietro's mother brought some of
his things to their house: a leather vest, an oval mirror, an iron
skillet, and a pair of shoes. Pietro found the shoes sitting evenly
in a corner of their kitchen; he stared at them for a long time, not-
ing the bumps and creases that had defined his grandfather's feet.

127

He reached over to pick them up and slip them onto his own sixteen-year-old feet, and found they were a good fit. Then he felt that one of the soles was loose, and that some of the stitching surrounding it was gone. He wanted to wear these shoes, to have them mended and polished. He was sure to get a few good years out of them. None of his own shoes felt so sturdy and sure. As he walked around the kitchen in them, he felt, he knew inside now, what it must have been like to be his grandfather; he began to know where his grandfather had been. All those stories about his travels to Roma and Napoli, to Pescara and Umbria, resided in those shoes. They would never leave him now, and he began to think about the places he might go in them, about where on Earth those railroads and great ocean liners would take him. Very soon, he thought, he would mend his grand-father's shoes. He would become himself a mender and maker of shoes, for they allowed you to go anywhere and do anything. They gave you confidence to bring the unexpected and unpredictable home. He knew now that that was what he would do.

MARK SABA grew up in Pittsburgh in a family rich in the traditions of both Italian and Polish heritage. He is the author of *Ghost Tracks: Stories of Pittsburgh Past* and *Two Novellas: A Luke of All Ages/Fire and Ice*, as well as the poetry books *Flowers in the Dark, Calling the Names,* and *Painting a Disappearing Canvas.* His fiction, poetry, and nonfiction have appeared in literary magazines and anthologies worldwide. He is also a painter and worked for 33 years as a medical illustrator and graphic designer at Yale University. You can view his creative work at *marksabawriter.com.*

DIASPORA

As "*diaspora*" *is the dispersion or spread of people from their original home-land, this book series takes its name in the intellectual spirit of willful dispersion of subject matter and thought. It is dedicated to publishing those studies and creative works that in various and sundry ways speak to or offer new methods of analysis and/or articulations of the Italian diaspora.*

Carmelo Fucarino. *Two Italian Geniuses in New York: Broken American Dreams*. ISBN 978-1-955995-05-4. 2023

Anthony Julian Tamburri, ed. *Re-Thinking* The Godfather *50 Years Later*. ISBN 978-1-955995-06-1. 2024

Anthony Socci. *United We Stand. Pre WW II-Chronicles of the Italian Colony of Stamford*. ISBN 978-1-955995-07-8. 2024

Antonio D'Alfonso. *I Could Have Been a Contender. (On Five Films)*. ISBN 978-1-955995-09-2. 2024

Antonio Vitti and Anthony Julian Tamburri, eds. *Studi mediterranei: bellezze e misteri. Mediterranean Studies: Beauty and Mystery*. ISBN 978-1-955995-10-8. 2024

Luigi Fontanella. *Bertgang. Fanatasia onirica.* Translation by Michael Palma. ISBN 978-1-955995-11-05. 2024. Poetry

CASA LAGO PRESS EDITORIAL GROUP

from CASA LAGO PRESS

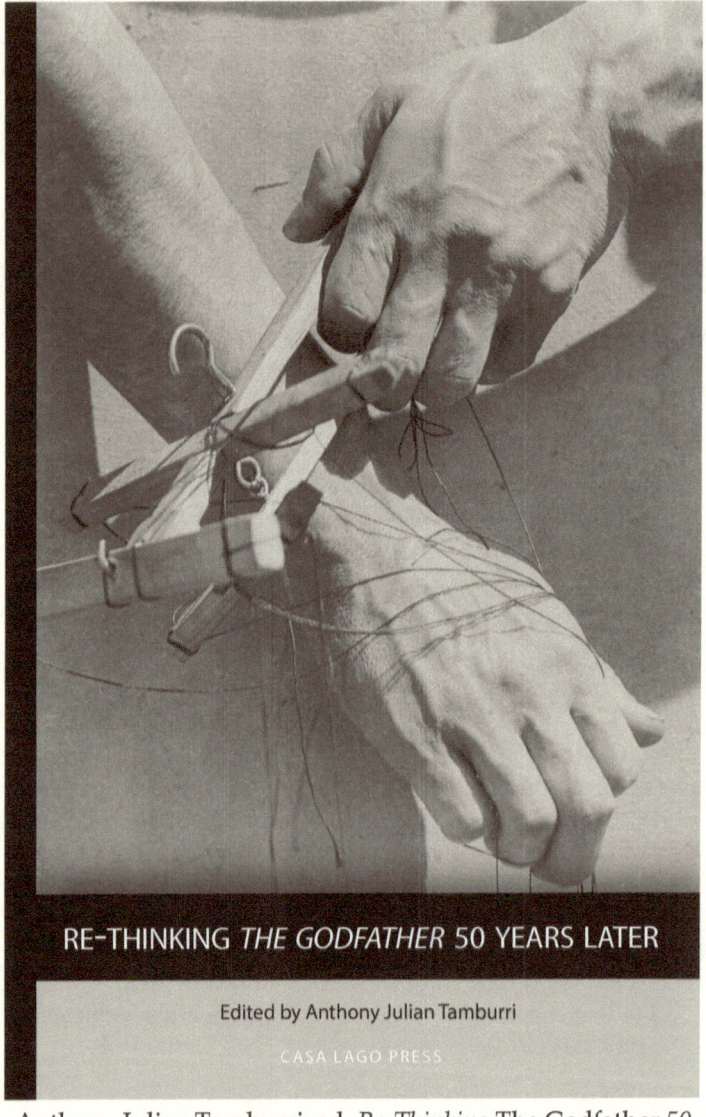

RE-THINKING *THE GODFATHER* 50 YEARS LATER

Edited by Anthony Julian Tamburri

CASA LAGO PRESS

Anthony Julian Tamburri, ed. *Re-Thinking* The Godfather *50 Years Later*. ISBN 978-1-955995-06-1. 2024.

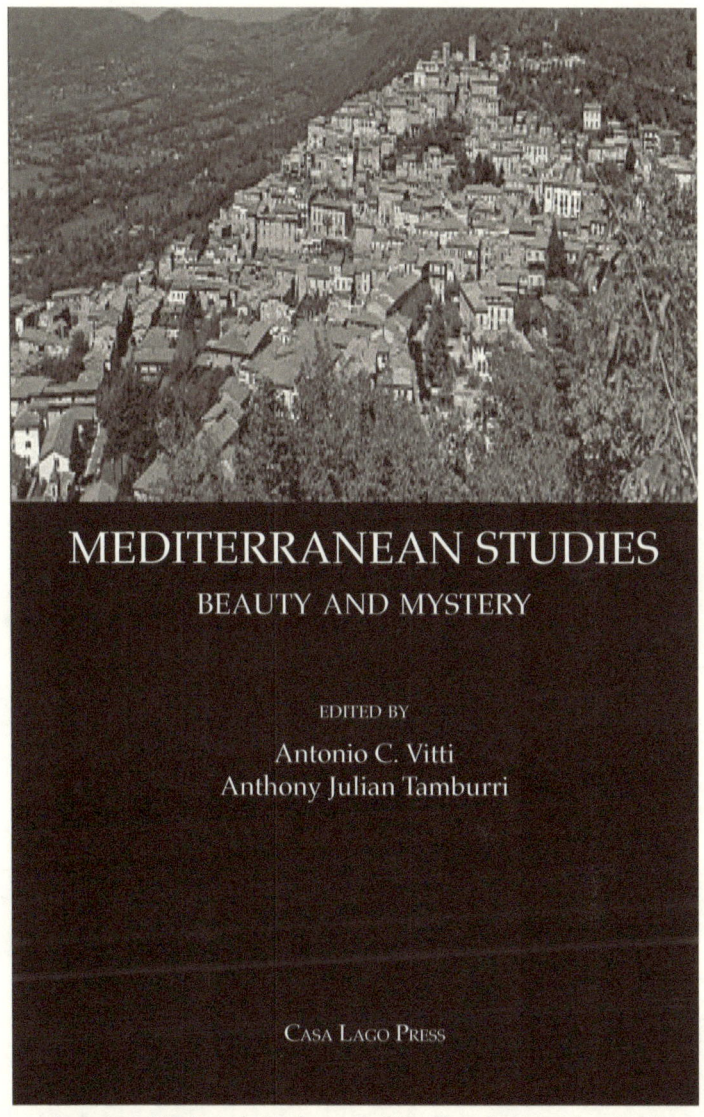

MEDITERRANEAN STUDIES

BEAUTY AND MYSTERY

EDITED BY

Antonio C. Vitti
Anthony Julian Tamburri

CASA LAGO PRESS

Antonio Vitti and Anthony Julian Tamburri, eds. *Studi mediterranei: bellezze e misteri. Mediterranean Studies: Beauty and Mystery.* ISBN 978-1-955995-10-8. 2024

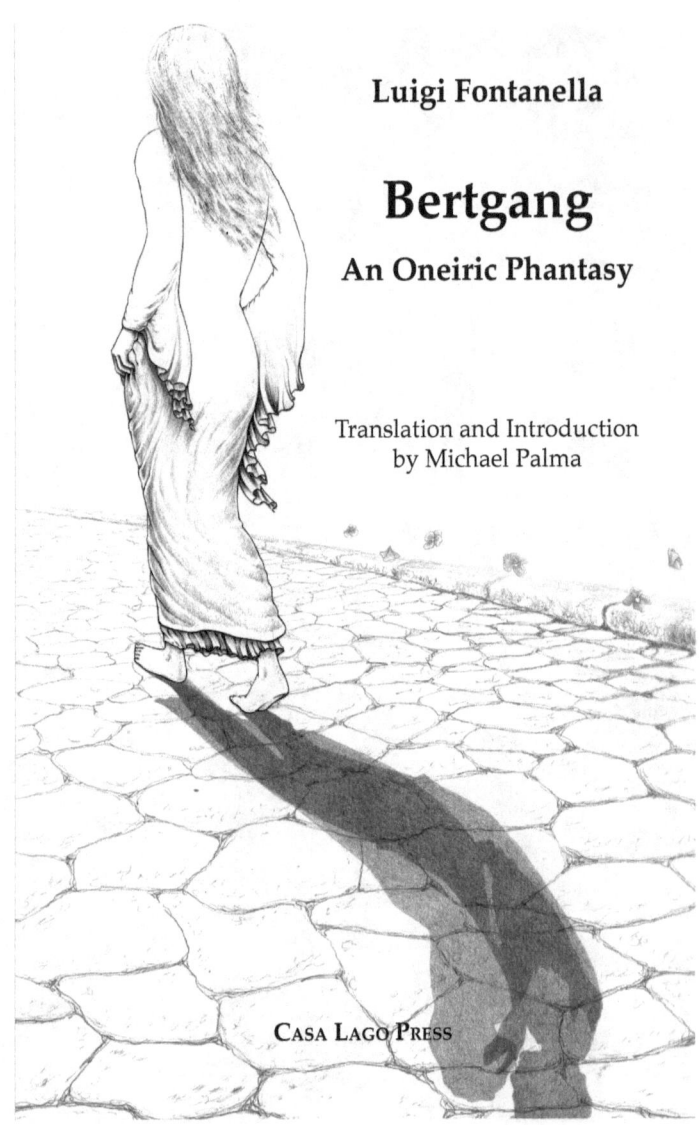

Luigi Fontanella

Bertgang

An Oneiric Phantasy

Translation and Introduction
by Michael Palma

C ASA L AGO P RESS

Luigi Fontanella. *Bertgang. Fanatasia onirica*. Translation by
Michael Palma. ISBN 978-1-955995-11-05. 2024. Poetry

www.ingramcontent.com/pod-product-compliance
Lightning Source LLC
Chambersburg PA
CBHW050758250626
47155CB00005B/2124